WRECKED

THE MERCILESS FEW MC

S Courtney

Cover by Linny Lawless (www.linnylawless.com)

Formatting by Zakrzewski Services (www.zakrzewskiservices.com)

Chapter One
Cullen AKA Reaper

The moment I hit that puddle-filled pothole while taking a curve, I knew it would be a disaster. I hydroplaned and hit my brakes... the wrong move. I leaned too much into the turn and lost control of my bike. I slid helplessly against the asphalt while my bike careened into a boulder on the side of the road. She bounced off and back across the street, pieces of her scattered everywhere.

That could have been me.

I was injured, but not as bad as slamming headfirst into a massive rock; no helmet would protect me from an impact like that. I slid for so long my gear was shredded when I stopped. Fortunately, a passerby coming from the other direction stopped and called 911. I remember losing consciousness as the paramedics tried to talk to me and then woke up in this bed. The attending nurse said my injuries could have been worse. I already knew that; I remember seeing the menacing 20-ton granite reminder staring back at me. Still, I was more concerned about the condition of my bike than knowing my DNA was now a permanent part of Highway 40.

"Get some rest, Mr. Anderson." The attending tells me after checking my IV and vitals.

"Call me Reaper."

He looks at me, checks the chart with his brows knitted, and scoffs, "You're lucky to be called anything, Mr. Anderson. I'll see you in the morning, don't give the night attendants any grief. You also have visitors; 45 minutes, no exceptions." He waves his finger at me. Whatever, the only bastards I know to come are my brothers.

I pull the thin white blanket up with my good arm to cover some of my injuries, but I can't hide the nasty road rash on the side and back of my bicep that ran up to my shoulder, but the worst of it is on my upper back and ass... to say I'm uncomfortable is a fucking understatement.

knock knock

"Come in!" I yell, forgetting it's a hospital.

The room fills with the laughs, wisecracks, and groans of my brothers, my club.

We are the Merciless Few: The Devil's Ignited Chapter, located close to Monument Mountain, near the sleepy town of Briarswood, Massachusetts.

Not a place you would expect a badass motorcycle club to reside, but the Merciless Few are everywhere. Our closest brotherhoods live in Rhode Island, New Hampshire, and Maine. But out of all of them, Maine is notorious. Don't let their isolation fool you; their location is prime for secret ship ports and unmarked roads. They are involved in it all, shipping and selling drugs, illegal gambling, drag races, and UFC-style fights damn near to the death. At least, I think. They were keen on using the seven deadly sins as a to-do list.

Anyway, my brothers fill the tiny room and give me a once over. I'm sure I look like shit; I feel like it.

Lucifer slaps my uninjured side. Thank God, but the look on his face told me he was in dad mode. Here we go...

He added to my pain when he slapped me upside the head, "Are you fucking mad?! Could've gotten yourself killed! How fast were you going? It was raining like crazy." I know he was conflicted at being pissed and concerned.

"I'm fine. Ass burns from road rash is all. Just need to get back to my bike and start repairing her, take my mind off of everything." I exhale angrily remembering why I was lying here.

Lucifer shakes his head frustratingly. My brother Wicked replaces him at my bedside. "Aye, maybe we should change your club name to Crash? You going to tell us what happened?"

I nod; to be real, it was a stupid case of cause and effect. So, I go into the pathetic story:

I had taken an impromptu ride to the neighboring town of Pleasant Point to see my girl, Daisy. She'd been bitching about not making an effort, claiming the club and my bike were more important than she was.

I hate to be the bearer of bad news, but I kept telling her to never force her place, to let it happen naturally. She was important to me, so here I was to surprise her and make her day. I wanted her to see that I was trying.

I made it to her house and she wasn't answering. When I turned to leave, I heard her voice somewhere around back, so I followed the sound.

"Yes, Liam, ooh yes! He never eats me out as good as you. He doesn't at all. I need this! Fuck yes, right there, don't stop!" I see her squirming and panting on the lounger splayed wide open with her next-door neighbor between her legs.

I'm sure he's had his sights on Daisy all along, and now he can have her. I let my guard down and cared for her, it may have hurt, but I wasn't going to show weakness.

Fuck her.

I cleared my throat; she went scrambling for her bathing suit leading me to believe she was probably tanning.

Her little boy toy hopped up fast trying to cover up; from what I saw, little was the perfect description for him. Eating her out may have been his only talent because I was at least twice his size and girth. I consistently pounded against her cervix, and she'd cry about how amazing I felt. I may not be the best at snatch licking, but I filled her well enough she didn't need pre-game. I didn't even mind her not swallowing me down her throat; her pussy was enough.

"Wait! Cullen, I..."

I hold my hand up, "Save your fucking breath, Daisy Mae. Enjoy that pencil dick loser." He flinched like I was going to hit him, I could. I could relocate his teeth to the back of his throat but he wasn't worth it and neither was she.

"Fine! You weren't the only one anyway! I've got a real man to take care of me!"

I know she wasn't talking about Mr. Right Next Door, which fueled my anger further. Angrily, I hopped on my bike and peeled out of there, leaving another useless whore in the dust. I let my emotions get to me and my focus wasn't on the road.

I fucking hate emotions and all that love bullshit. My love is my bike, my original old lady. When I saw her at the dealership, she sealed the deal of living the biker life, with my boots up in the breeze.

I come back to the present after relaying the story. I half expected to hear them cracking jokes or making fun, but not this time; instead, it was silence.

It's an awkward silence, so I break it, "It's fine. You told me she was another slut in a tight skirt..." I shift painfully, avoiding their judgments.

4

"Aye, then. We'll let you rest easy and sort out the lot, eh?" Wicked punches my good arm lightly as I nod, wondering how badly damaged my bike is.

Lucifer squeezes my shoulder. "Don't worry, Demon and Fiend will take the truck to pick her up from the pound. You can start working on her when they clear you."

Lucifer opens the door, and everyone follows him out. I placed my arm behind my head and winced; the stinging burn was excruciating; maybe I deserved to feel pain. I couldn't help to feel the self-pity.

I was glad they came alone; I couldn't bear to see Sam's motherly face after revealing the cause of my accident.

She married Lucifer and adjusted to taking care of her old man and his brothers, too. As the club mom, she and I would have intimate conversations. She told me she knew I was different. She said I felt and loved differently. I didn't screw the club sluts often, if at all, only when I was desperate to get off, and even then, I kept it cold and emotionless. No feelings involved.

"Cullen, you've got a big heart. Reaper is who you are to them; that macho bravado doesn't fool an old crow like me. My motherly instinct knows who you are. You'll find her someday; keep that big heart open, don't grow cold or worse, be like Asher. He'll never learn, jeez, that boy and those twins; he's going to lose his balls one day." She shakes her head, laughing.

Asher, aka Wicked, was the youngest in the club and by far the most reckless. He didn't have one girl; he had two, Priya & Tamla, the Amaree twins. They had no problem sharing everything, including him. You would hear the girls gossiping about how he was wicked in the sack; and that's how he got his club name. Their relationship was casual; he didn't claim or give them status; it was young kids having fun.

I wasn't much older, but Sam said my spirit was more mature and wiser. I'd be thirty this year and have had my fair share of life. Now my mindset wasn't my next lay, or even next girl. It was me, my bike, and our next adventure. I loved imagining where I would take her next. For a moment, that moment I forgot about my injuries and when I turned over to the wrong side, the stinging pain shot through me, and I hiss.

"Mother...fuck me!" I swiped the tray clean in response as a nurse walked in, stunned at my outburst.

She raised her brow to me. "Well, Mr. Anderson, I'm here to treat your road rash just in the nick of time, I see." She looked down at the cup and pitcher on the floor.

"My bad, I didn't think before turning over." She rolls her eyes as she gathers some paper towels and drops them on the floor. She places the cup and container back on the tray.

"You don't have to clean up after me."

She spread the towels as it soaks up the water.

"Who else is going to do it, huh? You're in no condition; don't make it a habit; I am not your maid." She's on her hands and knees, wiping around to get up as much liquid as possible. Now I was staring at her plump round ass in her teal scrubs. Her clean-up motions caused her top to shift, a lacy black thong peeking out from her pants. She was pretty, petite...and another woman, I relent. I didn't need that headache right now.

Suddenly, she clears her throat, and I shift my eyes to see she is watching me leer at her.

Shit!

I thought she would hand me my ass on a platter, but she only smiled. "Alright, mister, turn and pull your gown over so I can apply the balm and put on fresh bandages."

Great, I stare at her ass, now she has to treat the road rash on mine. I groan as I shift to reveal my injured side—even the cool breeze brings a stinging pain.

"Wow, that's brutal." I hear the snap of the latex gloves.

"From shoulder to the middle of your buttock, that must hurt." She held up a bottle I wasn't paying much attention to.

"Nothing I can't han....holy fucking shitballs!" I felt the sting of a thousand killer bees. I jumped and landed on the wrong side, causing more expletives to come flying out. "Fuuuuuuck, fuck, fucking son of a bitch! What the hell is that, battery acid on fire?!" I grip the sheets to keep from inadvertently choking her.

"Calm down; it's anti-bac spray. You don't want an infection, do you? And keep it down; it's after hours! I will apply a soothing gel before I bandage you up. It should help calm the irritation down."

I grit my teeth, "Fine."

The following day I was released. My very patient nurse, Bina, gave me plenty of ointment and bandages, she refrained from giving me the anti-bac spray and I silently rejoiced until she told me someone needed to replace my bandages every 24-48 hours. Longer than that, I risk infection.

That's going to go well with the guys, asking someone to cream my ass.

Wait. Don't say it like that...ever again...

I will ask Sam to do it; the bunnies will take that opportunity to try and hop on my dick. I'm like a needle in a haystack, and its bragging rights among them if they bagged me.

I will need to talk to Lucifer about letting Sam care for me. It's all about respect for the boss, asking for his old lady to nurse your wounds.

"So, what's your aftercare?" He looks over at me while puffing on a nice Robusto cigar as his breakfast.

I try not to wince at every pothole or bump we hit on the road. "Ahh shit, man! Could you take it easy?" He slows down, and I sigh in relief, "I needed to talk to you about that. The nurse says someone has to clean and bandage me every two days, and I wanted to see if you're okay with Sam doing it. I can't ask the guys to take care of my ass."

For fuck's sake, that sounds even worse.

He snorts and chuckles, "That's fine if it is with her. Somebody's got to take care of your ass, quite literally." Now he's full-on laughing, and I look out my window, ignoring the joke on me.

"So, how bad does my Betty girl look?"

Betty girl is my Harley Davidson low rider S with a custom midnight blue paint job. I knew restoring the paint alone would cost me at least two grand, but I've had her for four years, a gift to myself after proudly riding my dad's vintage wheels.

"She's pretty beat up. To be honest, it may be best to scrap her."

I shook my head; I wasn't ready to accept that. This would be more than your standard oil change. I've been maintaining her this long, I had to try to save the only girl 100% loyal to me.

Chapter Two
Avi

"Raven Samara, only a couple of toys! Hurry up, or we'll miss the boat!"

I am so sick and tired of unnecessarily suffering in this hell hole.

I'm sure the travel agents sell this location well. Brazil, known for its pristine white-sand beaches, thick Amazonian rainforest filled with lush greenery not seen anywhere else, and entrancing music-filled metropolitans, steadied by endless tourism income. Travel right outside Rio De Janeiro, a whole different world exists. Slums, crime, and violence run rampant in Maua.

I've seen it all, assaults, robberies, murders, and I've experienced worse. I've been beaten, assaulted, had too many guns pointed at my head, and all for the few *centavos* (cents) in my pocket.

No one is safe, and for that sole reason, I am fleeing this nightmare...for my precious girl. She doesn't deserve to live like this, she's already experienced so much trauma in her five years, and I won't stand another day. Only I can protect her, and I'll do anything to keep her safe.

My brother promised to send for us when he got settled in the States...that was three years ago. I haven't heard a fucking peep from that *mentiroso* (liar). I needed money to survive, and I had to beg Maurice, his lackey, to let me run between the lab and den, where they house it before shipment. He unzipped his pants in an unspoken demand. My back was against the wall.

After I gave him a blow job he had one other condition, I had to sleep and stay with him.

Before that, we stayed in the remnants of our parents' shack, with no lights and sometimes no running water. It was no place for a child, so I reluctantly agreed. It was one of my worst decisions in hindsight.

I continued to suffer physical abuse; even though it wasn't as bad as Raven's father, it was still more than I deserved. Her dad was another junkie dressed in fancy clothes; a monster disguised as a human being. I'm glad he's dead; I hope he's being spit-roasted in Hell.

I knew I had to get out when Maurice put his hands on Raven—smacking her for changing the channel on the TV. He hit her as if she owed him money. It was so hard she fell back into the wall. She didn't even cry, but the shock was evident in her eyes, and when she looked at me for an answer, I knew I had failed her as a mother.

That's why we are sailing out on the next shipment. We won't be alone; every shipment contains refugees looking for a better life.

"Mommy, can I bring my purpie blanket?"

She knows it's purple, but she giggles when she says purpie. Who am I to take away her little bit of happiness?

"Yes, sweetie, now hurry, the boat leaves very soon, and we

need to be on it." It could be another two weeks until the next boat left the port; time was of the essence.

"Where are we going, mommy?"

"We're going to see Uncle Frankie in the States, now come on and give me your bag."

She hands me her flower backpack, and I shine my flashlight to point out her purple receiving blanket.

I don't even remember the last time we had working electricity in this shack. I'll be glad when I can provide her with a decent home where she has her own bed with a frame and not a mattress on the floor that we share. Where she cradles me, not for warmth, but for nurture, and mommy doesn't have to sit up to make sure the rats don't attack her.

The first and only time she was two, I woke up to her screaming something awful and that's when I saw the rat gnawing on her foot. I beat it with a flashlight. I still have nightmares about it, and she has a distinctive bite mark on her toe. I rarely sleep for fear of time repeating itself. She doesn't remember, but I'm traumatized by it.

But in a week or so, we'll be in the land of opportunity, she deserves the world, and I'm going to give it to her, no matter what.

I take a final look...good riddance. *Deus nos proteja* (God protect us).

Chapter Three

Reaper

It's been a week since the accident. The guys did a few jobs without me but haven't cut me out of the profit, and I appreciate that because I need every penny to fix Betty girl.

We're contracted for armed security jobs, riding alongside private shipments to ensure they're not robbed on the way to their destination. What are they shipping? Most of the time, it's something illegal, like drugs or guns. One time we even guarded a pallet of gold bars.

But we draw the line at trafficking. No one should ever be taken or exploited for the sole purpose of making someone money, especially women and children. It is an absolute deal breaker and we always check the load before we're green to go.

Our journey usually begins when they offload these ship containers by crane and connect them to an 18-wheeler tractor. We get paid good money to escort these shipments locally, or to the border, then it's handed over to another security detail.

The refugees who hitch a ride on the boat usually stay in the area to find a way. They end up working for Frankie Cabrera, a notorious drug lord in town. He slithered in a few years ago from

South America, and his business exploded after his boss mysteriously disappeared, but Frankie probably killed him. After he assumed power, he ramped up production. We've done a few jobs for him, but he rubs me the wrong way, and I know I'm not wrong.

Since I've been home, Sam's been caring for me, although Dixie and Penny have been trying hard to keep her busy enough to offer me their...services. I'm sure it had a guaranteed happy ending, but Sam is sharp and onto their game, kicking them out of the house entirely when it's time to rewrap my wounds.

I hobble down the hall to see everyone eating breakfast. "Sit down, crash and burn. I'll fix you a plate." Fiend tells Demon to move as he sets a loaded plate down before I maneuver myself onto the soft cushion tied to the chair, courtesy of Sam. I see Lucifer eyeing me like a concerned dad would his son, and that's one of the best things I get from him. That fatherly love and support, as rough and rugged as we are, we're a family. A pretty fucked up family, but one, nonetheless.

He nods at me before Sam plops down in his lap and pulls on his beard while peppering him with kisses. They're like teenagers in love. Lucifer pats her ass which was her cue, time for club business. He motions his hand, and Fiend closes the shuttered doors as Lucifer calls for church.

"We got another job tonight, covering a shipment coming through on its way to Maryland. It's a small trailer, so I only need two of you. Wicked and Fiend, you're with me to make the first part of the trip before we hand it off to the next leg in Connecticut."

I lean forward but wince, the wounds are healing, but I'm still sore. "What do you want me to do, boss?"

"I want you to sit your ass down; you'll be back soon, don't rush it. We'll still cut you in, but for now, rest."

I slump back in the chair, defeated. "Who's the job for?"

"Our buddy, Frankie." He chuckles because he knows how I feel about him. Frankie's cocky and arrogant; he thinks he owns us to use at his will. In some ways he is right, but Frankie's sloppy. It's inevitable, he's going to go down hard. I didn't want to be burned by a man who wouldn't even save his family, let alone a group of bikers. I hope we find another contractor to cut ties.

I huff, "When are we going to stop associating with that bastard?"

"It's only business, Reap. I know exactly what he is all about. Don't worry I got us covered."

I'm not feeling confident, "He's an incompetent fucker who'd turn on us if it saved him from going to jail. He's a two-bit shyster."

"Is it that, or is it about him and Daisy?"

Oh, you heard him right.

Daisy is fucking Frankie now. Not sure if it just started or if she had been messing with him while we were together. Her little outburst allows me to assume the latter. It's probably out of desperation or spite; either way, it was another strike against Frankie.

Demon saw her with him down at the biker bar, Throttle. I asked if he was sure it was her, to which he produced a photo of her blowing him under the VIP table. That was how quickly she moved on from her carpet-munching neighbor a day or two ago. She probably used him to cum and left him hard and throbbing, jerking off to the fantasy of how close he was to fucking her.

But Frankie had money, status, and an endless supply to support her once occasional drug habit, which is now probably a full-blown addiction.

"Fuck her; this isn't about her and him; it's about him taking us down. I don't fucking trust him."

"So, you don't want your share of this job? I thought you wanted to get your girl back to riding condition?"

I fix her as much as possible before the pain overwhelms me and I need a break, but he's right; my girl needs a lot of work.

I retort, "You know I need that money."

"Right, and you don't even have to do anything." He smiles like he won the argument. "We will complete the job tonight, and tomorrow, we'll talk about the next steps for the charity ride and bonfire. Dismissed, we meet them at the checkpoint in an hour."

Demon stands up and stretches, "Well since I don't have to go, I'm headed to the bar to find a girl to slap my dick between her tits. Reaper, you coming?"

They didn't call him Demon for nothing. He didn't have a set of twins sharing him, but he was a cold bastard who liked to try out his BDSM fantasies, tainting those girls for life, especially after he discarded them like his used condoms. I don't think I've seen the same girl more than twice.

"Nah, I'm good. I'll be in the garage."

I'm sure I'll hear his victim leaving not too long after they finish.

Unless...he forgets to untie them again.

Long story short, we found her bound to his bed while he was in the shower. He came out after we banged on his bathroom door because he wore the key around his neck, and from then on out, he promised to at least release them back into the wild before hopping in the shower.

What the fuck, man...

I stand up slowly to gain my footing, sighing hard when the wounds feel like they are cracking open with every movement.

Wrecked

I groan as I shuffle like an old man outside. I whistle at my baby like she is the most beautiful woman in the world. Even though she was damaged, she was still gorgeous. "My Betty girl, let's replace those shocks today." I lift the frame high enough so I can work on it.

Chapter Four
Avi

We made it to the docks. They shuffled us into a clean container and left the door open for ventilation. There were about 50 men, women, and children.

Raven kicked off her sparkly pink tennis shoes and laid across my lap, knocked out in seconds with her purple blanket. I didn't realize how late it was until I checked; it was 2 a.m. I continue to brush her hair as the distance between our nightmare widens and our new start begins.

I sighed, relieved to be getting away, but there was one detail I hadn't quite worked out, how would I even know where to find my brother?

He abandoned us, his sister, and his niece. How could he forget *a familia dele?!* (his family) Maybe I'll start over, but how? As much as I hated to admit it, I needed my brother.

I had plenty of time to think about possible solutions as we drifted into the depths of the Atlantic on our way to the States. Perhaps by then, I would have a course of action that doesn't include selling my body. What I gave to Maurice was enough of my soul sacrificed to *o proprio diabo.* (the devil himself) I wasn't giving another ounce. There had to be another way, a better way.

I find myself keeping watch as my little angel sleeps, but eventually, I doze off. I'm only rattled by the low groan of the ship's foghorn before I fall back asleep. Not only dreaming of a better day but sailing toward it.

Daylight breaks over the waves, no land in sight. The seas were calm but, at any time, could turn treacherous; I was praying for traveling mercies. Some migrants were sitting outside the containers enjoying the crisp, salty sea air.

"*Mamae?*" (mama) I hear my sweet little girl call for me as she walks out of the container; her legs are a little shaky from the ship's movement, but she makes her way and finally falls into my lap, giggling. I open my bag and hand her a *rolo de pao* (bread roll) with some ham, and a juice box. I take a roll for myself and watch her smile at nothing. "*Mamae*, how long will it take to get to the States?"

"It's going to take a while, sweetie. We'll have to make do until we get there. At least there are kids on the ship to play with; just stay away from the edge. We have some snacks, and the crew of the ship told me they have plenty of food in their kitchen, and we are welcome to join them at any time. Do you want to see if they have some fruit to go with your sandwich?" She shakes her head, "No, I want to be here with you, *mamae*." She leans against me, and I can't help but smile and kiss her forehead. One day down, several more to go...

Chapter Five

Reaper

I thought I wouldn't have to see Frankie's smug face for a while, but here he is at our clubhouse, 'celebrating' another successful handoff of his supply. He never wanted to celebrate before, but suddenly he wanted to.

He strolled in wearing his overly expensive but poorly fitted suit. The scantily clad girls dispersed from his presence and started flirting with all the guys, including the monkeys he brought with him. I can't be sure, but they're either girls from his strip club or prostitutes, likely both.

Daisy was all over Frankie, giggling, pretending I didn't exist, but it was all for show. I knew what they were doing, and he definitely wanted to rub it in that he was banging her.

Fuck both of them; besides, she wasn't looking well. The heavy drug use was apparent, her skin looked dull and she looked unhealthily thinner. She was a shell of her former self. I guess that's what happens when you're ugly on the inside.

Lucifer steps in front of me, "Hey, I didn't know he would bring her. You alright? I can shut this down."

Am I okay looking at the reason I slammed my precious bike into a boulder in the rain?

"I'm fine, she belongs to the streets. Shutting it down only proves I'm bothered and I'm not." Lucifer nods hesitantly as my eyes meet Frankie's cocky, arrogant gaze. I sip my beer and head to the bar.

"Thank you again for ensuring my shipment made it across state lines. To the Merciless Few! The best money can buy, isn't that right, sweetheart?" He holds up his drink; Daisy looks at me, "Sure thing, baby. Can we go? I'm horny."

She said that to get a reaction, so I did. I stood and watched her eye my 6′ 3″ frame. I took that moment to adjust my seven inches soft. Her eyes followed, and she licked her lips, probably reliving the times I fucked her unconscious from too many orgasms.

I sat on the barstool and whistled Lila over; she knew the distinct sharp tone, almost like a mating call. Her eyes met mine in confirmation and I nodded affirmatively. Lila was a club bunny, but she wasn't desperate like the others. A bonus, she fucking hated Daisy.

Daisy tried to claim queen bee status and demanded we eliminate the club 'sluts'. That didn't go over well with the fellas or the girls.

Lila stepped in her face, she was a good five inches shorter than Daisy, but her confidence was ten feet tall. "You may have a slightly higher status than us, honey, but you'll never be an ol' lady...at least not his." She raised her brow while winking at me and turned around to walk away. Daisy shrieked as she lunged at Lila, but Sam caught her by the neck, slamming her against the nearest wall.

"This is MY house and those are MY boys! You will not disrespect anyone welcome here, do you understand me? Get some sense or get the fuck out! Reaper, handle your bitch, or I'll gladly do it for you." Sam shoved her in my direction with so much anger. It was one of the few times Sam lost her patience and honestly, I was scared for both of us.

That night, Daisy played victim as she sobbed in my arms in my room and even while I drove her home, her chest heaving against my back. I had to persuade her that she was still my favorite girl. I convinced her five times, leaving her passed out and satisfied. From then on, I met Daisy at her house or in town.

Now she was in our clubhouse with that dickhead. He always found a way to rile me up and this time was no different as he headed my way. Lila paused her movement to watch it unfold. She waited to strike while the iron was hot.

"Ahh, Reaper, it's so good to see you."

Why the fuck is he talking to me?

He continues to babble on, "Oh, what happened there? Did you crash your little bike and get hurt?" He waves his hand toward my road rash. I looked at Daisy, watching her put two and two together and realized it may have been her fault.

Let me drive the point home.

"Yeah, that's what happens when you let your emotions get the best of you. No worries, it wasn't even worth it, not in the least bit. Have a good night."

I got up slowly, enough for him to retort, "I'm sure we will, isn't that right, my little Daisy Mae?" I saw her freeze up when I glared at her. I was the only person to call her that; she hated her middle name, but she said it was cute when I said it. It was supposed to be a special bond between us. Guess that was a lie, too. I exhale loudly but don't say anything as I head to my room.

I slam the door and groan loudly, missing the sound of my door opening again.

"Hey, don't let that skank get to you. She looks terrible and definitely leveled down to be with the likes of him."

Lila hops up on the dresser, swinging her legs in her daisy dukes and boots. She looked like a southern belle with her red plaid shirt tied to showcase her ruby belly button ring. She observed me and I could feel her judging me but also trying to comfort me.

"Forget about her. She's not meant to be with such a great guy. Leave her in the gutter with him where she belongs."

"I thought I loved her, Lil..." I whisper because no matter how tough I try to act, it stings. Still, I didn't want pity.

She sighs and sits beside me, taking my hand, "Nobody should have their heart broken like that. I'm... sorry. Listen, even though you don't deal with us club girls like that, I'm here if you ever feel the need to take out your anger with some rough kinky sex. I won't beg you, but I'm here." She laughs and nudges my shoulder, which makes me chuckle. I wrap my good arm around her waist and she pokes my side. Thankful it wasn't where my rash was and she leaned her head against my shoulder. She was a great friend. We never went down that road, but I won't lie and say I wasn't curious. She was a firecracker and girls like that liked to pull surprises in bed. Besides, she is the only girl here who dealt with Demon and walked out of his room without a scratch.

Back to the present, we both jumped when my door opened and Daisy stood there.

"I was...umm... checking on you. I know Frankie can be vindictive and..." I could tell by her continuously looking back that she had snuck away to come find me.

Lila slides into my lap, wiggling her ass at the same time. She's itching for Daisy to say something. I wrap my arms around her, it stings like hell, but I don't let it show. I nibbled and placed kisses on her shoulder.

"Oh, don't you worry about him, darlin'. I'm about to make him forget all about you. Isn't that right, Cullen?" Her calling me by my real name established that she was more than a piece of ass. Law states all club girls were to call us by our club name unless we said otherwise.

"Now, would you close the door unless you want to watch him fuck me like a rabbit?" That was the final dagger; Daisy's eyes grew wide and filled with tears before she turned on her heels and left the door open. Lila slides off and leans against my arm again, laughing.

"I knew it would piss her off if I called you by your real name. She deserved it. Listen, you will find that girl you can't stop thinking about, who brings sunshine into your life, and knows what she has. She's somewhere Reap, don't give up, okay?" She smashes her finger against my forehead, putting some silliness in a serious moment.

"Yeah, you're right. Thanks, Lil, for everything." I tap her ass, so she stands. After that impromptu lap dance, I need a cold shower before Sam comes and does our after-care routine. The sessions are faster now. We're trying to allow the wounds to get some air. Only the parts that were still seeping were bandaged back up to avoid infection.

Tomorrow will be an extended maintenance day, she's almost rideable, but a new fear emerges... will I even have the courage to hop back on and put my boots up?

Chapter Six
Avi

It's been a long week, but it is still better than living with Maurice or in the slums. Raven has adapted well and even found herself a few friends, two girls and a boy around her age. I think the boy may have a little crush on her; it's innocent and cute. It's normal and not predatory, I never liked any male near her because the chances of abuse were high. If I wasn't working, she was with me at all times.

It was 10 p.m. when I saw my first glimmer of hope from the opening of the container, a rotating beam of light. I knew it had to be a lighthouse that signaled boats safely to shore. Wherever we are supposed to dock is close, and I notice more little lights dot the shoreline. Raven had just fallen asleep beside me. The boat crew had been so nice to us, they gave her a blanket and a pillow to make it more comfortable. I was still guarding her as I did at home, but I was getting more and more sleep each day. I look forward to eight hours of sleep, which will be the night I place my *princesa* (princess) in her own bed in her room.

Before I left, I managed to snag $500 US from Maurice. I

didn't steal it; I deserved it after the torment he put me through! It wouldn't last long, and I would need to find my brother for help and fast.

I slipped out of the container to get a better view of the land slowly revealing itself through the fog. One of the parents stood beside me.

"Hey Avi, why aren't you asleep?" He put his foot up on the rope mooring, rocking back and forth with his hands in his pockets.

"I never slept at home. I was always on guard, you know? Bad habits die hard. Why are you up, Cruz?"

He kicks a rock over the edge, "I'm praying I can find work to support my family. What about you? Do you have a plan?"

"Sort of, my brother is already in the States, and I am going to find him. Hopefully, he will help us until I can get on my feet. I don't want to live off of him just enough so Raven has a decent chance."

horn blare

It was so sudden I lost my balance for a moment before I caught myself, but Cruz held his arms out in case I didn't. Knowing I was okay he starts to laugh. "We must be about to dock. We better get in the container. I'm not sure if they have customs or not; better safe than sorry." I agree and we head back, letting everyone know to keep quiet. The kids were sleeping soundly so that decreased our chances substantially.

Wherever we were docking, I was about to take my first steps toward freedom. Although I'm still angry, I hope I'll be happy to see my brother. To have what's left of my family.

Two hours later

. . .

Wrecked

We get off after the crew comes and tells us there were no customs or police around. Since it was midnight, we were offered free room and board at this hostel off the shore by the dock. Everyone would have their own space and that was my first sign of hope.

When we walk in, we are greeted by a middle age woman with the sweetest smile, "Welcome to Massachusetts. Make sure you sign here, please. I know you're ready for a hot shower and a nice soft bed. My name is Melissa, if you need anything, don't hesitate to ask."

When it's my turn to sign in, I ask, "Do you know who Frankie Cabrera is?" I didn't expect her to know anything, but I had to start somewhere.

Her blue eyes went wide like I asked about a notorious serial killer. "Yeah, he runs the syndicate here, drugs, trafficking, you name it. Why do you want to get involved with someone like that?"

I shrug, "I don't, but he's my brother. I have to start somewhere."

"Oh, dear. Well, he lives in a gated mansion a few miles from here. He usually inspects his shipments the morning after they arrive. If he has anything on that boat, then he'll be here around 7 a.m."

I gave her an appreciative smile as she handed me the key. Raven is still rubbing her eyes; I'll put her right to bed and figure out what I want to say to my dearest brother.

Chapter Seven
Reaper

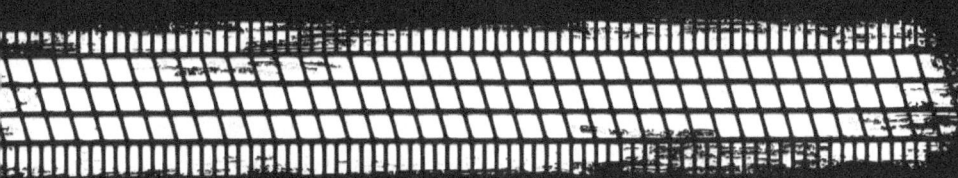

She needs some dents knocked out and a fresh coat of paint, and then I'll be able to test her out.

But my stomach churns at the thought, what if I can never ride again? The excitement and adrenaline I once felt are replaced by crippling anxiety.

I'm so deep in my thoughts I don't see Lucifer seated beside me as I tighten the brake pads.

"Feeling apprehensive to ride?"

I didn't say anything to anyone, but he seemed to figure it out.

"How did you..."

"It's natural to feel that way after an accident. Remember when I told you I traded in my truck for my bike after I flipped it three times? I never wanted to drive a truck again, but now I am comfortable using it when I need to. My advice is to start with a short ride down the driveway and back then work your way further."

"I feel like a burden because I can't help with the jobs and we're still dealing with Frankie to keep the club running."

"We're still dealing with him for the money, that's it. And you're not a burden; you're our brother. One thing at a time; we'll take you riding when you feel up to it. Take my old girl, Maxine, but only when you're ready. I'll let you get back to work. I got a gal named Sam and I'm ready to smack her ass and hear her squeal." He groans while I cringe; they're like my parents.

Nobody wants to hear their dad talk about banging their mom.

I looked over at his first bike, a simple 2005 Harley 1200, she may have racked up some mileage, but he treated and cleaned her so well that she looked impeccable to be so dated. Perhaps I will take him up on his offer. Betty girl has to go to the body shop for last-minute fixes before hitting the paint shop. I won't see her for at least two weeks, and I need to get my bearings back...for her.

Chapter Eight
Avi

I took a much-needed shower before waking Raven and getting her ready to see her uncle. She hadn't seen him since she was a toddler. I'm not sure if she even remembers him. I put her in a short-sleeved sunflower dress and black capri pants, pulling her hair into pigtails and matching bows. She shuffled in her shoes because they made a clicking noise, making her laugh. "*Mamae, are we going to see tio?*"

"We are. Are you excited to see him?" She jumped up and down, saying, "Yah" repeatedly until I put her backpack on and grabbed my bag. I hope I can keep my anger at bay.

It was 6:48 a.m. when I made it back to the dock and we sat on a bench near the ship. Raven regaled me with all her knowledge of the ocean, some she already knew and stuff she picked up while reading on the boat. She was going to excel in school here; I felt it.

I notice a caravan of black sedans and SUVs pull up near the dock. A big buff guy in a suit steps out and opens the back door to the SUV and my brother emerges.

Jeez, he's been eating well.

He buttons his suit and holds his hand out, then a woman steps out, and the security guy closes the door. She wrapped her arms around him and I could already tell she'd be trouble. Women can be territorial when they don't have a rock-solid foundation and my guess is she's nothing more than easy access. For her, there's nothing scarier than another woman trying to establish herself in the man's life and she becomes forgotten. But I'm his sister, I outrank her, but I didn't want anything more than a bit of support while navigating this new life.

She was going to get defensive, but I didn't give a shit. She looked like a common *prostituta* (prostitute). Who wore something that skimpy this early in the morning, or did they not go to sleep? She looks like she reeks of cheap booze, used condoms, and motel sheets.

He stepped onto the dock, pointing at the ship we stowed away on, "Yeah, the shipment came in early this morning. About a quarter mil once we get it broken down and packaged. Then, babydoll, I'll take you shopping for whatever you want."

"Really, Frankie?! I want a big shiny diamond ring!" She held her hand up, but he stopped immediately. His expression is now a scowl. "I told you I don't do marriage. I'm married to my work; if you can't accept that, I'll find another girl who knows her place. Got it?"

She recoiled at his words and nodded. "Maybe a new wardrobe for the summer, Frankie?" He nodded and she was smiling like she was on top of the world again.

I stand in the middle of the dock and wait for him to recognize us.

The girl stops when she sees me and her face says it all. Raven shoots out of my grasp and runs towards him, *"Tio, tio! It's me! It's me!"* He bends down, so she runs into his arms and he picks her up.

"Raven, *meu raio de sol,* (my sunshine) you've gotten so big!"

"I'm this many now." She holds up five fingers. He kisses her cheek and hugs her before laying his eyes on me. I think he knew to tread lightly because he had to explain himself eventually, but right now, my baby girl was happy, and I wouldn't tarnish that.

"Frankie."

"Avi, it's so good to see you," He smiles.

Fucking liar.

"When did you get here?" He pats me on the shoulder, disguising it as a pathetic attempt at a hug.

"Last night. Apparently, on one of your shipments from home."

"Oh, okay, cool. Well, where are you staying?"

"We don't know. Let's cut to the chase; I'm not here to bleed you dry before any assumptions are made," I eye her because that's precisely what that bitch was thinking. "I need stability to get on my feet, that's it. We won't be any trouble, Frankie, please! I had to get her out of there. I'd rather die than go back home."

She scoffs and he removes his arm from hers while cradling Raven, who had surprisingly fallen asleep. "You can stay with me. I have a few bedrooms you can choose from for you both."

"No, she sleeps with me. Thank you, Frankie, thank you." He nods as I follow behind him.

"Diesel, Rex, handle the shipment. I've got to take *minha familia* (my family) home. Make sure those pea-brained neanderthal bikers get my shipment to where the fuck it needs to go. Daisy, you ride in the sedan."

She gasped as her mouth fell open. I could tell she already felt she was being replaced. I also knew if I stayed too long, something terrible would happen.

35

Eventually, we pulled up to this massive estate; it was red brick with white shutters. The driveway circled and we stopped at the door. Frankie scooted as he maneuvered to get out while he kept Raven in his arms; she slept the whole way here. I'm startled by a door slamming behind me as Miss Priss huffs, her heels banging against the cobblestone. She almost broke her ankle trying to express her hostility, but it only made her look desperate for his attention. He could do much better than some drug-addicted trash.

Inside, he showed me everything on the way down the hallway to the left. "There are three guest bedrooms. You pick which one." I opened the first one on the right. It didn't matter; I would make it work. The room was a soft rose gold theme and he set Raven on the king-size bed. I pull her backpack and shoes off and lay her purple blanket over her.

He signals for me to follow him out. Guess it was straight down to business. You have no idea how long I've been waiting for this, *irmão*. (brother)

Chapter Nine
Reaper

I've been taking short rides a few miles and back. Even the sight of the bike outside of the barn has my heart racing and I get flashes of the accident and worse flashes of what could have happened. When I finally get the nerve to sit down my hands shake and I can't get a good grip. I'm drenched in sweat and still anxious. They say I look stiff and uncomfortable. I am and the healing doesn't help because the motion causes it to open up and along comes the stinging and burning. Sam always slathers on a layer of soothing gel after every ride.

I'm on the mend though. Besides the sore parts, the road rash is peeling and looks like a pink tattoo against my tan skin. You could tell I'd been in a wreck, especially in a short sleeve.

It'll be the talk at the annual B.A.C.A. charity event. B.A.C.A. stands for Bikers Against Child Abuse; every year, they sponsor a 50-mile ride in each region and end it with a giant bonfire. This year we're hosting the bonfire for the Northeast. It's a few weeks away, but we're already prepping for a huge crowd. It'll be bikers, booze, and BBQ.

And we'll be sloshed off our asses if we drink from old

Josiah, the town's master moonshiner. He likes to concoct the bathtub brew and the way he tells the process makes him sound like a mad scientist. He usually makes a batch and lets it "settle" for a month to ensure maximum effect. So, there's no doubt he has already made a big batch for our event.

If we're not too plastered, we'll have a touch football tourney and, of course, a wet t-shirt contest. Sam said she's participating and is in it to win it, that weirds me out. She's our club mother; pretty sure I don't want to see her tits. I'm not even sure what sorcery she pulled to convince Lucifer to let her compete. He's a notoriously jealous man and she's a radiant beauty.

Hopefully, no one will make any trouble. I've seen Lucifer crack a man's jaw for disrespecting her. The guy and his friends were drunk at Throttle and he was bold enough to smack her on the ass. She didn't have time to react before his head snapped back from Lucifer's left jab. He wailed on him for only about 15 seconds, but it was enough that he had to have his jaw wired shut. He probably could have killed him in 30 seconds. Like I said, notoriously jealous.

Finally, at the end of the night, we write the check for all the money raised and hand it over to the B.A.C.A. organizers. We may have rivalries and sometimes feud with each other but there's one thing we will never tolerate and that is abuse against women and children.

I'm brought out of my thoughts by tapping at the garage door. I look up to see Sam.

"Hey, kiddo, what 'cha doin'?"

"Polishing Maxine. Betty girl cost me two grand at the body and paint shop."

"Yikes! Well, you'll be back to your old self and routine in no time." I see hopefulness in her eyes.

"I'm not too sure about that, Sam. That wreck changed me

and I don't recognize myself. I wonder if I'll ever ride again or if..." I hate to admit this. Sam gently touches my arm and it spills out.

"Daisy hurt me. I thought I loved her and now she's sleazing it up with Frankie... I never want to get that close again. Did I deserve this? She said I didn't show her enough..."

"Stop it! Don't 'pity party' yourself. She's a slut who chose money. If she cared or loved you, you would have worked it out. She didn't even try, she hopped on the next available dick. You didn't deserve any of it, but it happened for a reason. You'll get comfortable riding again and soon, some little firecracker will grab your attention and she'll be the luckiest girl in the world. Get through these dark times and you'll see that I'm right. Mama always is." She laughs while hugging me from behind.

If only I could be so optimistic.

Chapter Ten

Avi

As we enter his office, he snaps his fingers and his security leaves. He sits at his desk and observes me, he thinks he still knows me, but years of abuse leave me quiet, but short-tempered. I have a daughter now and she looks up to me, so I lean back in my chair and stare back until he breaks, "I'm sorry I didn't send for you."

"I'm sure you are."

"Avi..."

"No, you see, you expect me to regale you with wonderful times about my days, weeks, months with your sorry-ass lackey Maurice. Not about how I suffered physical, mental, and verbal abuse to ensure your niece had a roof over her head and food in her stomach!"

Hmm, maybe the old me is still there.

"I had to shack up with a man I wouldn't let touch me in public. The things he made me do behind closed doors... but I endured it because I thought my dear brother would eventually rescue me because I was his *familia.* (family) How fucking wrong I was! Years later, I realized I got to do this myself, he wasn't thinking about his sister or his niece and when Maurice put his hands on MY daughter, it was now or spend my life in jail after killing that worthless, limp-dicked bastard with a fucking butter knife! Being abused, beaten, and held at gunpoint numerous times was nothing...NOTHING compared to feeling abandoned by you! You want the truth?! I thought you left us for dead! You were wealthy and well off here with your bimbo and I'm telling you now, I will not hesitate to shove my fist down her fucking throat if she comes at me disrespectfully. I'm not here to latch on and suck you dry like her, Raven deserves a chance and if that means working for you, then I'll do it."

I didn't realize I had stood up and was leaning forward. I gathered myself and sat back down. His face was still expressionless and cold.

He had changed, and I didn't recognize my sweet, loving big brother anymore. He clears his throat and stands, "You'll start tomorrow and get what they get. No special treatment or extra because you're my sister. This is my business, *estamos entendidos?* (Are we clear?)

I nod as he continues past me towards the door. "You can be a girl in my club or a runner between businesses."

"You would trick out your sister?" He didn't have to say sex worker or prostitute but they weren't there just serving drinks.

"It's just business, sis. Besides, you already did with Maurice; what's the difference now? You could make premium money for that p..."

I reared back and slapped him as hard as I could. "That was for survival, *seu covarde de merda!*" (you fucking coward)

I stormed out of his office towards my new space, leaving with no answer. I was devastated to see what he had become and how money had changed him.

That monster was not my brother.

Wrecked

Fighting the tears and the urge to slam the door, I see Raven unpacking the bags. She folded all her clothes as best she could and put all the dirty ones in a pile. She was humming while walking toward the open drawer in the dresser.

"What are you doing, sunshine?"

"I'm putting our clothes away, mommy, so you don't have to. Did you see the bathroom?! It's bigger than the whole wide world! Can I take a bath tonight, *mamae*?"

She never had that luxury; it was a shower, or I'd have to plop her in the sink. A few times I had to bathe her in the ocean.

"Sure, and I'll add lots of bubbles." She squealed in excitement. Then someone knocked on the door. A tall, lanky gentleman in a suit opened the door and stood there. "Madam, lunch is prepared. Follow me." I signal Raven to hold my hand. She stares at the man; she's hesitant about any new man, and I blame myself. He smiles and bows to her, causing her to giggle, putting her at ease as we follow him through this huge mansion. I could only describe this house as palatial; it was overly extravagant and a testament to his selfishness. Filling the place with priceless treasure and compensating for everything we couldn't afford back home.

We entered the dining area, where the double doors were opened. Frankie's seated at the head of this room-length table. He could easily host a party of 30 people. He sips his coffee while Miss Priss eats tiny bites of food. She huffs when she sees me. His response to my arrival was to rub his face where I hit him. He only felt a fraction of my hurt.

"*Tio! Tio!* Your house is so big! It's a pretty fairytale castle!"

"Thank you, sweetie. Put your napkin in your lap."

"And thank you for my room. I will sleep well after my bath."

Finally.

I see the excitement on her face, looking forward to being dipped in warm, soapy water as I scrub her squeaky clean. Then, falling fast asleep, not having a care in the world. It made me smile, but that was short-lived when I realized he was staring at me. I coaxed her to eat her strawberry pancakes and bacon while ignoring him. She told me everything tasted terrific, pointing to certain plates and I gave her small portions for her tiny size. I knew her eyes were definitely bigger than her stomach. Afterward, I'd take her out back and let her run around.

"Do you have any pets, *tio*?" She asks between bites.

"Don't talk with food in your mouth. Yes, I have two dogs, but they aren't for playing. I do have an aviary with some birds. You can take a look after you've finished eating if it's okay with your mother."

Then the biggest set of brown eyes focus on me. "Of course, you may, after you finish your plate." She swings her legs happily as she cleans her plate.

I'm annoyed he keeps trying to correct her manners, she's a child, and her manners are fine. I keep my focus on her and my plate. My wrath still boils on the inside from our earlier conversation, but I know I must give him an answer.

"Done! May I go see the *pássaros* (*birds*), *mamae*?"

"Piedmont can escort you there." Piedmont was the butler's name. He holds his hand out and Raven happily accepts after their quirky moment earlier before breakfast. She immediately starts to ask him a ton of questions. I hope his patience is high. It has to be to work for my brother.

"Daisy, don't you have to be at the club soon?" He raises his brow. "Go wash last night off you, you smell like a used condom."

I chuckle because I said that, but I don't look in their direction. The chair scrapes against the floor as she stands up abruptly. "Hmph!"

Now I'm alone with him. I stand and his eyes follow. "I will do any task that does not involve sex. You have your answer."

"Avi..."

"What, Frannie?"

"Don't call me that."

Don't call him that... I couldn't say it right when I was a kid and that's how I called for him. It wasn't until junior high when he said he was too cool for that and then I used it to tease him. Only when he pissed me off, like now.

"What, afraid of a connection to your old life? Sorry, I wouldn't want to bring up anything that would embarrass Frankie the badass."

I scoff as I walk away. I didn't realize he was behind me until he grabbed my arm, squeezing tightly. I try to snatch away, but he grips tighter.

"Don't patronize me, Avi. You will respect me! I have a reputation to uphold and I'm your ticket to your bit of freedom."

"Wouldn't want to ruin your precious reputation here as king of the crack whores. At least feed the *cadela magricela*." (scrawny bitch)

I snatch away successfully to find my little bit of relief in this hell.

After her luxurious bath, complete with a pink sparkly bath bomb and brushing her hair until she falls asleep, I hear a tap before Frankie steps in.

"Take this payment to the Merciless Few motorcycle club now. It's their final payment for the last run. Diesel will take you to make sure you do it right."

He tosses the envelope enough for me to catch. I make sure Raven is comfortable before changing into a black tank and blue jeans, pulling my hair up into a ponytail and slipping on my sandals. I flick on the night light and kiss her cheek before slowly shutting the bedroom door. I pray she stays asleep. Walking towards the front door, I see Diesel eyeing me.

Sem chance no inferno. (no chance in hell)

I walked past and slid into his elevated truck. Frankie's standing there waiting for us to leave. Diesel gets in and smirks, "Hang on, sweetheart, this baby's got some kick." He felt like he was saying something so impressive that I couldn't wait to hop on his dick. I rolled my eyes and looked out the window as he hit the gas. The tires screech as we rear up on the back tires before returning to the ground firmly.

My first official task was to pay off some slovenly group of dirty bikers. Of course, Frankie kept company with the bottom feeders.

We made it to this large two-story, fraternity-style home in the backwoods somewhere. It definitely could use a new coat of paint. It was decent for the type of people that live here. I open the door to see Diesel ready to help me down. It was a lousy attempt at a cheap feel and I was already in a bad mood. I hop down on my own and I hear him close the door.

I walk up and knock; Diesel is right behind me. I can feel his breath on my neck. I snarl, "Why are you so close?! Back up, or I'll twist your balls off and feed them to the dogs."

He chuckles, "I like a chase, sweetheart. Your brother said you were fair game, and I can't wait to feel that tight little pussy around my dick."

Frankie said, what?!

He's offering me up to his lackeys like a fresh prostitute and I am livid. I'd slit Frankie's throat in his sleep if I didn't need him. He doesn't give a shit about me and right now, the feeling's fucking mutual. The way I'm feeling, his flunky here is about to have a very agonizing sex change.

"I don't give a damn what he told you! Don't fucking touch me, you mongrel." In my anger, I slam my fist against the door three times. I probably sounded like the police, but I didn't give a shit. Somebody better answer before I commit murder on their doorstep.

"Alright, wait a damn minute!" A voice on the other side yells out. The door swings open and I'm staring at a nearly naked beast of a man, but I'm really ogling his bare chest, a nice one at that, except my eye is drawn to fresh scars on his arm that look like they wrap around his back. They are pinkish against his warm skin. I was so fascinated I failed to see the irritation on his face until I looked up and he sneered, "What?!" He stares down at me.

"What?! Don't they teach you basic manners to address people when answering the damn door, or is it true what they say about bikers? Nothing but a bunch of brainless Neanderthals."

Everyone was pissing me off tonight.

He looks behind me and recognizes Diesel, "Hey, Frankie letting his whores deliver payment now?" He taunted as he snatched the envelope. He was about to slam the door in my face, but I wasn't going to tolerate disrespect.

I stuck my foot in the way and put my arms up against the door frame, "Despite your ignorant statement, you seem like a decent guy, quite out of place to be a mangy, trashy biker, but what do I know, huh? You might be as bad as my brother Frankie. I'm not some *vagabundo* (tramp) like that *cadela* (bitch) he's dragging around like a fucking trophy. I don't know why, she looks like any other $10 whore, but whatever. IF there is a next time, I suggest you show me some respect, *seu idiota covarde!*" (you spineless prick)

He raised his brow and shifted his weight while rubbing his chin, the muscles automatically flexing in his chest and arms.

He was also in his boxers; I wonder if I interrupted his sleep or a good time? I could hear female voices from behind the door.

"Did you call me a prick?"

Oh shit. I didn't expect him to understand me!!

I didn't know what to do! I squeak out a 'sorry' and promptly make my retreat...

Stupid, Avi, stupid!

Chapter Eleven
Reaper

I picked up a bit of Portuguese from casual conversations at the bars with the migrants. So, when that little fireball called me a spineless prick, I repeated it and all the color drained from her face. It was cute.

Honestly, I got a kick out of her insulting Daisy, but she hightailed it back to the truck before I could react. She had a pretty nice ass. I wave the envelope at Diesel before closing the door. Another dirty deal with the Devil in the books.

A beautiful girl verbally assaulting me was a great way to end my night. My body didn't seem to mind, though. In fact, it made me hard as a rock. I love those no nonsense, smart mouth women, they tell exactly how they feel with no filter.

No way jerking off is going to do the job tonight. I needed to hear someone panting, moaning, screaming my name. I needed to feel that unmistakable warmth and that moment she shatters underneath me. I'm considering Lila's offer for a quickie. I needed to forget all my problems: my crash and burn, my Betty girl being repaired, Daisy whoring it up with

Frankie...and now add the hot-headed firestorm that sparked my interest.

But she's another woman, another headache you don't need. My brain insists, but...

Is she?

I shut the door and the girls at the high table were eyeing me like a steak. I realized that my erection was visible and growing. I had rolled out of bed to answer the door. I was the only one who was not occupied. You could hear multiple screams of pleasure throughout the house; it was like we were shooting simultaneous porn films.

The remaining bunnies were waiting for their turn. We had more girls than guys, but that's because Demon and Fiend were known to be greedy, with multiple partners in one night and even though he had the twins, Wicked was known to sample a different dessert from time to time.

I could see hope in all their eyes, hope that I would finally take a chance with one of them. All except Lila, who was typing on her phone.

What the hell?

"Come on, Lil. Tonight's your lucky night."

She hopped off her seat, teasing with her hot pink thong pulled up over the top of her shorts she had unbuttoned and folded down with her ass peeking out. She sauntered toward me and wrapped her arm around my waist. She barely came up to my stomach. I lean forward, wrap my arm around her, and hoist her onto my waist. "Well, I never thought I'd see the day!"

I catch her off guard her with a kiss while grabbing her ass, making her squeal. "I'm hard as a rock and I know it'll take more than my hand to get rid of it and you offered...."

"That I did. I bet it was that spicy little minx at the door. She sounded super-hot. Tell me, how insanely jealous are they that I bagged the unicorn?" She smirked and I looked behind her to see the envy on their faces.

"Come on, I'm ready to fuck you senseless. Maybe you can teach me the best way to eat pussy...even if it takes all night." That caused a few lip bites and shifting in their seats, their pussies throbbing at the thought of a man soaking his beard with their orgasm and not stopping.

She rubbed herself against me, "Mmm, fuck...I like the sound of that. Well, let the lesson begin. Night, ladies," She remarked smugly as we left.

When we reach my room, I toss her on the bed. And for a moment, the doubt creeps up. "Lil..." I start to back track.

She rolls her eyes, "It's just sex, Reaper. An outlet for your emotions, I know what this is and we're friends. Friends help each other out and besides..." She pulls off her white crop top, exposing her tits, squeezing them together and letting them bounce. Then her hand slips into her thong and she licks her fingers. "I'm soaking wet and you need to make me cum...hard."

Shit. Well, she did offer and after that aggressive confrontation at the front door, I need this. I didn't respond to her comment about the girl being hot. She didn't need an answer, my dick told my truth and now I needed to relieve the tension.

I dropped my boxers and she watched as my dick thumped against my stomach. She eyed me hungrily as her tongue traced her lips.

"Suck it." I didn't need to say more as she slid off the bed and knelt before me. She looked so innocent, but then she stuck out her tongue like she was receiving communion, except I was blessing her with the taste of my dick.

I spanked it against her warm wet tongue; the air hitting the wetness made me shudder. Her tiny hand wraps around it and she puts her lips close to the tip and pauses. She looks at me and winks; the next thing I know, she inhales and sucks me in. The feeling is fucking unbelievable.

"Shit, Lil, ease up a bit." I wanted to enjoy the moment, but she shook her head defiantly and started bobbing her head. I couldn't stop the freight train if I wanted to. I shot a load down her throat and she swallowed it all. Opening her mouth to show me her disappearing act.

I had to lean against the dresser because she almost brought me to my knees. She took that opportunity to peel out of everything else and lay in my bed spreadeagle.

"Come on, you want a lesson in eating pussy? Class is in session...it'll give you time to recover." She smirks, teasing herself while waiting for me. I'm mesmerized by her movements, lost in her moans of my name, then she beckons me to lay between her legs.

I got a crash course that night. Lil made sure I knew everything. How to listen to a woman, that she'll give you clues of what she likes and what drives her wild. That a good indicator is her hands in your hair, the tighter the pull, the deeper and faster you go. I devoured her like ice cream in a bowl with no spoon. She was compensated with multiple orgasms and I was rewarded with another mind-numbing blow job. After that, we were both too exhausted to even fuck, but both very satisfied.

She smirked at me and I kissed her forehead, "Thank you, Lil."

"Anytime. Well, maybe. I need to improve my endurance because if you eat like that, you probably fuck like a rabbit."

"I've fucked Daisy unconscious, so it's a possibility."

"Yeah, but she's like a wet mop. Wispy and frail."

"Says the girl who tapped out before sex."

"Looking at your soft dick, I'd say you're pretty tapped out yourself."

"Fair. I didn't expect the lesson to be so thorough."

Suddenly, she gets up and starts getting dressed. "Where are you going?"

She turns around and musses my hair. "I was here to expend some energy. I'm going to Throttle to grab drinks with the girls who didn't get lucky tonight. I know they're dying to hear deets about me bagging the unicorn."

"Do you guys really refer to me as that?"

"Yup! Who else has bagged you besides me?" She had a point and then she placed her hand on my face. "Hey, I'm here anytime, but remember, the girl of your dreams is out there. You got to keep this open." She points at my heart before she punches my arm and hops up.

"See ya later." She nods as she walks out. I lay there with my hands behind my head. I just gotta keep it open; easier said than done. I head into the bathroom to remove my bandages and put ointment on what I can reach. Sam was busy at the moment.

Chapter Twelve

Avi

Diesel confirmed to Frankie I had completed my first task. He eyed me and nodded before walking away.

You're fucking welcome, ingrate.

"I'll be at the club." He spoke as he walked out, I didn't know which one of us he was talking to, but it didn't matter. I turn to head to my room, but Diesel grabs my arm and I snap, "For the last fucking time, don't ever touch me again, or I'll slice your dick lengthwise and shove it down your throat. I'm not a whore or free access. I'm here for my daughter; this is your only warning, *filho da puta,* (motherfucker) you got it?!" I realize I might need to start carrying a switchblade again. I'm not safe here, either.

I didn't wait for his answer as I made it to my room and locked the door. I was relieved to see my baby had found her way under the covers, holding onto her blanket, and sleeping peacefully. She hadn't panicked but instead snuggled herself into the luxurious sheets and soft pillows to possibly have the best night of sleep in her life, which made all this worth it. I retire to the bathroom to wash the night off before pulling her into me and joining her in sweet dreams.

"*Mamae. Mamae*, wake up. It's morning time!" I feel the bed bounce as I open one eye to see her playfully jump up and down, giggling.

"*Bom Dia*, (good morning) sweetheart. No more jumping." I looked at the alarm clock, it was 8 am, but it felt like I had only slept for two hours. Either way, I had to get up. I needed to find out how I was getting paid and how often, which required interaction with my brother.

I'm sure he was looking forward to me coming and begging for money, even though it was money I earned—I'm a burden in his eyes. For him, I was better off left to fend for myself in Maua, out of sight, out of mind.

Like before, he was at the head of the table. This time he wasn't reading a paper but enjoying what was on his plate. His plastic trophy wasn't around, which was nice, but Diesel was seated in her place. Not sure if my threat worked, I guess time will tell.

"*Bom*...I mean, good morning, Uncle Frankie! I've been practicing my English for school." Raven skipped ahead of me to sit close to her uncle. I reluctantly sat next to her.

"You sound better, sweetie. Keep practicing every day and you won't be teased for sounding different. Maybe we'll go shopping for some clothes and uniforms today."

I didn't like his condescending tone and negativity, she sounded just fine. Before I could decline his offer, she bounced up and down excitedly. "Yay! Mommy, Uncle Frankie's taking me shopping." I grit my teeth, "That's nice, sweetie." I could see she was practicing her English, calling me mommy. She's been bilingual since she could talk. I knew she would eventually need to learn English if we were still in Maua or elsewhere. Most jobs required or preferred English speakers and paid better.

Once she ate, she went to clean up.

I turn to Frankie, "When do I get paid?"

He chuckled and Diesel followed suit. "Quite eager for $200, are you? You'd average $800 a night if you worked at the club. More if you provide special services."

"I'd pay a pretty penny to get those lips around my dick." Diesel growled.

I ignored my urge to tell Diesel to go fuck himself and look at Frankie, "I told you no the first time. I'll run your errands and collect payments, but I am not some whore! Now give me what you owe me!" I stared him down until he snapped his fingers and Diesel produced a wad of cash. "You heard her; pay her share." He pulls out two hundred dollar bills and holds them out enough where I would have to bend over the table to reach. I snatch and put them in my back pocket while he gawks.

"Watch your attitude, Avi. I won't warn you again."

"Whatever." I went to check on Raven. I could hear the water running in the bathroom. I put the $200 in her stuffed bear with a small rip in it. I decided that's where I'd hide the money until I could open a bank account. "Raven quit playing in the water and get ready to go with your uncle."

"Okay, mama!"

She comes out smiling, hugs me, and kisses my cheek. "Love you, *mamae*."

"Love you, too, bug!" I attack her with tickles and she screams while trying to get away. We walk out to see him at the front door. "Ready?" She releases from my grasp and runs to him. "Yeah! Yeah! I'll be good, mama."

"I know, sweetie, have fun."

Frankie looks at me coldly, "You have several runs to complete. Diesel has the list. Keep it up, you'll have a pretty penny, but there are faster ways..." I know he wanted to continue that statement, but I think my expression stopped him from bringing it up in front of my daughter.

He cleared his throat to break the intensity, "Come on, let's go shopping."

"Yay, shopping! Bye, mama!"

"Have a good time, sweetheart."

Back to business I suppose. Let's get this over with, "Where's the first job?" I was hoping not to have to go back to that biker house. I was still mortified and mildly turned on from the last encounter. I have to admit...he was fucking hot.

"We got a few drop-offs and some collections." He opens the door and gestures for me to exit. His gentlemanly action makes me suspicious but as long as he's not hitting on or touching me.

The first three were drop-offs at his staging houses, where they'll break the massive bricks down for dealer distribution. I got flashbacks of Maurice every time some sleazy guy accepted his delivery. I'd get the money before Diesel handed over those huge bricks with strict instructions and the approximate net value when we come back to collect. The first guy handed over $150,000 in one of those bank security bags. The second had a smaller payout of $40,000, but he was assigned to a smaller area. The last guy was an even smaller operation but generated over $10,000. Three pickups and Frankie was already $200,000 richer; here I was making three percent of that.

The silence in the car was distressing, so I asked the burning question, "How much do you make per job?"

He glanced at me before shifting his hands on the steering wheel, "You know what they say about curiosity, Avi."

"Spare me your lecture. I know my brother is lowballing me to get me to work in his strip club, but I won't do it. So, spill it."

"Alright, I make $5,000 a job." He looks over and shrugs.

What I could do with that kind of money, I'd only need to

do a handful to live comfortably while I looked for real work, but my brother is feeding me scraps, barely enough to survive. It's a power move, stating you need me more than I need you and you'll get what I give you and like it. He expects me to happily accept with a smile and not ask for more than he is giving.

Like when we were kids, he'd give me the blueberry and cherry pieces from the sugus pack because he didn't like them. I thought he was a good big brother and sharing. It wasn't until junior high when my friend gave me a bag, did I discover there were three other flavors!

I continue to stare out the window until we get back, keeping my frustration to myself. Frankie and Raven were sitting in the living room watching cartoons. He has this massive, almost circular cream sofa and Raven had her shoes kicked off and was kneeling, rocking to the music of some American children's show singing about the continents of the world. She seemed to catch on very quickly.

She glanced over, "Mommy, look, I know the words now! Australia, Asia, and America, too! North and South because there are two!" I feel so much joy watching her so bright and full of hope.

"That's very good, sweetie!" Frankie kisses her temple, "Back to work for me, kiddo. If you want a snack, ask Piedmont, but be polite." Another etiquette tip from Uncle Frankie but I keep to myself.

"Okay." She replies as she scoots back.

He motions for us to follow him to his office. I set the money on his desk. "$200,000 collected from three vendors. I'll take my $600 and be on my way."

"It's only $300."

"What?! You said it was $200 a job, Frankie! That was three jobs!"

He sat back and lit a cigar, "I did, but I also spent money on my niece. You're lucky I only took half; you should be in debt to me. Take your money and go."

He tosses the money and it slides to the end of the desk. "You would charge me... for taking your niece shopping? It was your idea; I didn't ask you to take her!" I felt the lump in my throat, but I would not give him the satisfaction of seeing my tears.

"She ain't my kid. But she is family, and you can't provide for her, but it also won't be for free. Everything is business."

"I'm sure it is. Excuse me."

I rush to my room, shut the door and slide down, letting the pain flow down my cheeks. What did I do to deserve this? All I want is the best for my little girl, nothing more. I don't want anything for myself. I can't let him break my spirit; I can't. I wipe my tears away and look for her stuffed bear to add today's meager earnings. I sigh hard as I clutch the bear to my chest.

I'm conflicted by my brother's behavior: I know I am lucky to be earning anything but I'm also so angry at how cold and condescending he is to his own family.

Then a knock startled me when Diesel came in. I think he could tell I had been crying.

"What do you want? I'm not in the mood right now."

He walks toward me and it makes me uncomfortable. I realized, by sheer size, I could never fight him; he could easily overpower me. Maybe he won't take no for an answer. I watch as he reaches into his pocket and pulls out a stack of bills.

"Here. Take one of my shares for today. You need it more than me."

He can't be serious?

"I couldn't. You don't have to do this, really. I was so nasty to you." Trying to hand it back but he holds up his hand.

"You did threaten to slice my dick up and shove it down my

throat, but you were being protective. I know you want better for that little princess out there. You reminded me of my mom when she busted her ass to provide for my sister and me. I would never let a woman work herself to death if I can help it. Now, take this and put it towards a better life. I make enough and it's only me. I don't plan on working for your brother much longer anyway."

"Really?"

"Yeah, you see, there's this girl I've been talking to online, but she lives in California."

When he spoke about her, I watched this big, menacing guy turn into a teddy bear. I was shocked.

"So then, why were you constantly hitting on me when you clearly have someone waiting on you?"

"It's a front! The tough guy, macho bravado act I put on for Frankie. I would never force myself on anyone. My mama would have done to me what you threatened." He laughs and it's almost like I'm looking at a completely different person.

"You seem like a cool person, Diesel. You should lead with that instead."

"My name is Herschel."

I slap my hand over my mouth to stop the laughter, I manage to choke it down. "No way...let's umm...let's stick with Diesel."

"That's cold, Avi." He wipes a tear from my cheek. "Do whatever it takes to give her a better life but be true to your boundaries. She deserves it...YOU deserve it. Alright?" I nod as he nudges my chin then pulls me into a hug. This is weird and comforting. He pulls back and looks me over.

"Thank you...Herschel." I couldn't help laughing; it didn't fit his demeanor.

"Oh, haha. See, this is why I go by Diesel. I'm going to do my rounds before grabbing a late lunch. See you later."

I couldn't help the smile forming as I held that large wad of cash. I was lightyears ahead of schedule. I put a hundred in my wallet and the rest stashed away. I removed some of the bear's filling to make room and cover it back up. I came into my room heartbroken but walked out hopeful. I was closer to my goal of getting away from my corrupted brother.

Chapter Thirteen
Reaper

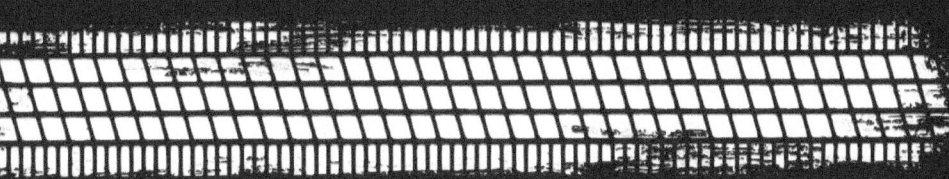

The boys, minus Lucifer, drag my ass out the house to Throttle on a Friday night. They're trying to take my mind off of everything, distracting me with loud music, booze, and women. Fiend watches me slam down half a beer in one go while he sips his. "Aye mate, you gotta take it easy on yourself." Maybe I am being too hard on myself, pitying myself and putting all the blame on me. It's easier that way.

Wicked is in the booth beside us with Priya and Tamla all over him. He was slouched down and both girls had a hand disappearing into his lap. He looked very pleased as they took turns shoving their tongues down his throat. Truth be told, he could have stayed home instead of witnessing a live sex show.

I turn back and watch the girls on the dance floor, giving them the attention they're vying for. Demon growls before I catch him eyeing his next victim, a tall Nordic beauty at the bar in a tight graphic tee and leather skirt, right up his alley.

"Look at those tits, perfect to squeeze my dick between and have her suck the tip. I'm picturing... leather neck-to-wrist restraints and nipple clamps tonight. She looks like a screamer, too. 'Scuse me."

Thanks for the visual. I'm wound up again but haven't seen Lil since that night. I was wondering if she was avoiding me. Then I see her dancing on some dude, grinding her hips against him as he pulls her harder against him, guess that answers my question.

Seems she's been busy and that's cool. She did a friend a favor, but that's all it was. I finish my beer and go to get the next round.

"Hey, Stitch, another round for the boys and a shot of Jack." The bartender nods as he prepares my order.

"Hey sexy, you must be new in town. You one of Frankie's new girls? How much you charging, sweetheart? We can go somewhere..." A gruff voice catches my attention, especially when he mentions that bastard.

"Don't you understand no? *Recuar! (back off)*"

I know that attitude. I see the same firecracker that was banging on our door boxed in against the bar by this huge guy who was too drunk for his own good.

He leans closer to her neck and inhales, "Mmm, you smell damn good...I bet your pussy tastes even better. Why don't you hop on the back of my bike and go to my place?"

"Are you hard of fucking hearing?! Back the fuck off me! Do you American pigs not understand what no means? It's the same language."

He reaches behind her and pulls her hair so she's looking up at him and his other hand has both her hands in his so she can't fight back.

"I heard you, but that's not the answer I'm accepting." She stomps on his foot to get him to release, but he doesn't; in fact, he pulls her hair tighter and forces his lips on hers. She squeals trying hard to get free.

Wrecked

The switch flipped and I stormed over, got my arm around his thick neck to get him into a chokehold, and once he let go of her, I tightened my grip. "Did you not fucking hear her the first time? Leave, or I'll slam your fucking face into the bar, they'll have to feed your fat ass through a straw!"

I shove him hard and he falls to his knees before returning to his feet. He turns around, "Who the fuck do you..." His words die when he sees not only me but my club emblem on my cut and my brothers behind me. Even Wicked had jumped up from his booth to join the impending brawl. I wanted that motherfucker to jump stupid, I've been looking for a way to violently disperse my anger. I could tell that my reaction was a culmination of everything that's happened. My emotions are unpredictable right now. The drunk holds his hands up and backs away until he disappears out of view.

I see her rubbing her scalp as Stitch starts to place my order in front of us. I place my hand over hers, "Hey, you okay?" I thought I'd get an answer, but instead, I get a pissed-off-looking woman who smacks my hand away.

"Why are you touching me?! I didn't need your help! I'm sick of all these men thinking I'm weak. I can take care of myself, *idiota*!" (asshole)

That was it; I cage her in like he did, but I smirk because I saw her breathing hitch and her eyes become wide. "First, I'm a prick and now I'm an asshole? Do you ever think you might come off as a hot-headed judgmental bitch? I'm not the enemy, sweetheart, so don't direct your anger at me. A thank you would be the proper response to someone saving your ass."

Her nostrils flare and her chest was heaving. I'm not sure if she's irate or turned on. I was definitely turned on by our exchange. I backed off and stared her down. I already knew she wasn't going to bend easily, not after the first interaction. She proved me right when she rolled her eyes. Then she looks over, grabs my shot, and downs it before slamming the glass.

"Thanks... for the drink." She shoves me out of the way as she disappears into the crowd. I stand there blindsided momentarily, trying to figure out what just happened. Stitch replaces my shot, "No charge, hero." I'm joined at the bar by the fellas as they grab their beers. "Who was that, Reap?" Fiend asks me.

"You remember someone beating on the door a few nights ago like the cops? Maybe you don't because you were busy. I answered the door and Diesel was there with her and they were dropping off our payment from Frankie, the weasel. I thought she was one of his new whores. Turns out that's his sister."

"That's his sister?! Where's he been hiding her?"

"Judging by how thick her accent is, I don't think she's been here long. Our first interaction wasn't the best, I was pissed I had to get out of bed, so I answered the door angrily and she didn't take it well. Called me a prick in Portuguese and I called her on it. She squeaked and turned tail." I shrug my shoulders and take a pull of my beer.

Fiend raises his brow, "Ahh, now it makes sense."

"What?"

"The damn heat between you. You'd have to be blind not to see it. It was a mutual eye fucking. Face it, you want her badly."

"You're crazy if you believe that. She couldn't wait to get away and I'm glad she's gone. I don't need the headache."

"Uh-huh. I'm headed back to the house."

I nodded as I leaned against the bar, reaching for my wallet and pulling out $50 to pay for the round of drinks.

"While you're paying, stud, order me a dirty little slut." I look over to see Lil smiling while sitting on the barstool, swinging her legs. I roll my eyes and slip another twenty out of my wallet.

"Add a dirty little slut for the lady." I lean against the bar looking at the crowd trying to avoid her gaze.

"So...already replacing me as a fuck buddy?"

"We haven't even fucked, so I don't see how that's possible. Besides, what happened to that blonde dude who was all over you?"

"You mean Peter, my friend, who happens to be gay?" She chuckles, which makes me laugh. "I thought you were avoiding me and regretting what happened." She reaches for her drink, "Nope, no regrets at all. Flashbacks got me through a few nights of masturbation. Anyway, I was helping Peter move and decorate his new place, that's all. But it looks like I should be the jealous one. Who was the feisty new girl? Was that the same chick from a couple days ago? I saw the sparks from here, but I get it. She's hot. I'd bang her."

My mind conjures up a steamy scenario I'm not ready for. Could you imagine? Both of them naked in my bed teasing me while they rub their pussies together, panting until they cum all over each other before beckoning me to join them. I shake myself out of my fantasy to see her sly smirk.

"What is everyone talking about? She hates my guts and has called me everything under the sun. I don't feel the attraction. Besides, she's Frankie's sister; I don't want any affiliation with that dirty bastard. Good riddance to him and her."

She grabs my dick and chuckles when I freeze up. "Your dick says differently. It says you want to pound her sweet pussy til the sun comes up and she can't even whisper your name from cumming so much. Face it, Fiend is right; you got it bad."

"I do not." I stutter out. I'm lying through my fucking teeth. I choke down my beer and slam the bottle harder than I should.

Score one point for Lil.

I also realize she's still slow stroking me under the bar. I already feel close. "Lil…" I try not to let my voice waver, but she's got me by the balls.

"Are you ready to take out your frustration? I think you owe me from the last time and you need to practice what you learned. She'll thank me later when she's writhing under you."

I started to say that she was crazy if she thought I'd ever be involved with the likes of her, but she pressed her thumb down on the tip and all I could think about was needing to cum. She bites her lip and pulls me down so we're eye to eye, "You can call me by her name." She lets go entirely and turns towards the bar, finishing up her drink. She hops down and leads me out the bar.

I'm so riled up I could barely think straight. Two confrontations with that smart-mouthed little hellion and each time left me stiff as a board. Right now, I only care about getting my dick wet besides…

I don't know her name.

Chapter Fourteen

Avi

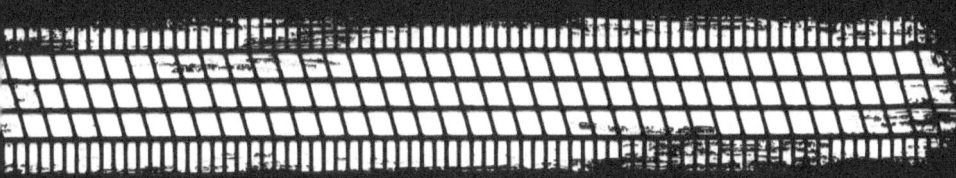

Porra! (Fuck) I slam the front door and immediately regret it. I stay still for a moment, listening for movement. After hearing none, I exhale loudly, running my fingers through my hair.

Why did Frankie send me to that sleazy bar alone? He wanted me to drop off a brick to the owner and collect $10,000 from the last drop-off. Who knew so little product brought in so much, I assume it's because he can charge whatever he wanted with no competition.

I walk towards his office to drop off the payment and collect my fee. I am still fired up from another confrontation with that dirty, blonde grease monkey. What's his deal? I'm not some weak little girl. I can take care of myself. Then I stop and let the whole situation sink in. Nobody else seemed to care about that mutt that was harassing me after I clearly said no. It could have ended badly. I was in trouble with that drunk pervert and I'm glad he was there. I don't know his name. I only recognize him by the road rash marking his muscular arm. I should have said thank you, but my pride got in the way.

Stupid, Avi, stupid!

And for that, he called me a judgmental bitch. Maybe I am. I locked away my heart and feelings long ago after I felt a hand across my face the first time. Women are abused by every male figure in their life back in the slums. We're never safe. I was so sad when I gave birth to Raven. Not because I didn't love her but because if I stayed, I knew her chances of being abused and molested were high. And when Maurice hit her, I heard the clock ticking toward more and more abuse. I won't let her go through what I went through.

I'll die first.

I couldn't wait to check on my munchkin; she was reading in bed before I left. Her current fascination was now all sea life. After discovering the depths of the seas and how only a tiny percentage of the waters have been explored, she's been dying to learn about the lesser-known creatures. She's my little Einstein.

I take longer strides to finish my job so I can take a relaxing shower. I didn't knock; I walked in to see Frankie sitting at his desk.

I walk up and toss the bag on his desk. "Here's your payment from the biker bar," I saw him bite his hand before he leaned forward. He looked uncomfortable. "Good and you dropped off the next batch?"

No, Frannie, I kept it for myself.

"Of course." He sighs, then gasps but clears his throat to try to cover it up. He was acting strange.

"You, okay?"

"Don't ask stupid questions. I-I'm fine." Then he gripped the desk before trying to concentrate enough to reach for his wallet in his back pocket, making him wince. I raise my brow as he opens it and pulls a wad of 20s.

"Take it and go." He tosses it and slams his wallet on his desk in frustration, I think. I could tell he overpaid me, but I wasn't going to point out his mistake. Besides, he'll realize later and dock me. It's better to stash it now.

I stared for a moment, then turned around after I confirmed it when I heard that distinct noise.

"Get out, Avi!" He barked; I guess I wasn't moving fast enough.

I start counting my money on the way out. "Fine, Frannie. I suggest you tell your *vagabunda* (slut) to cover her teeth with her lips when she's sucking your dick. A tip, honey, no man likes sharp teeth scraping up their dick. Can't crack whores remove their teeth and place them in a glass?" As suspected, she shot up, ready to mince words, but I chuckled while walking out.

The way he was wincing she was scratching him up good, or her bony hands were like sandpaper sliding up and down. I don't know how she makes any money at the club...then again, I don't care.

I walk from his office to my room. I see his security making their rounds outside. That comforts me that she's safe when I'm not here. I step inside our room and my angel is snuggled up with one of her books in the middle of the bed. I gently separate it from her grasp and use her unicorn bookmark, so she doesn't lose her place and set it on the nightstand. I kiss her forehead and grab some pajamas to take to the bathroom.

If Frankie did one thing, he bought the best of everything, which is evident throughout his house. Our guest bathroom was massive, with a garden tub and a rainforest shower with a bench. I let the hot water run, creating a sauna. I rub my sore neck and realize how long it's been since I've been touched or had pleasurable sex. With Maurice, it was a chore. There was a short stint with a close friend, Corbin, he showed me the affection I longed for, and I finally felt beautiful and attractive to someone.

And the only reason I thought about it was for a split second; I felt that attractiveness again when he pinned me against the bar. The heat radiating off his body from the anger was intoxicating. I fantasized it was only him and me in the club. One hand pulled my hair back to force me to look up while his other hand cupped my jaw. It slid across my chin, down between my breasts. His intense gaze dared me to look anywhere but in his eyes. Then I felt his fingers separate and end up around my nipple, which stiffened in anticipation. I hold my breath waiting for the pain when he squeezes, but he merely brushes it and it causes me to gasp. I didn't expect such a feather-light touch.

He leaned closer, his breath brushing against my lips. I found myself pursing my lips, silently begging for him to take me. He leaned even closer and then chuckled before backing off.

"Say please, baby girl..." He catches me off guard by squeezing my nipple like I imagined, further fanning the flames.

"Please...please." I'm so aroused in my fantasy that I mimic his movements in real-time. His hand slides down my stomach, heading for my pussy which is now dripping wet. His fingertips trace around my stomach, to my hips, squeezing my ass before returning to my lower abdomen; his movements are slower, more methodical...torturous...until I finally feel the electricity of his..."

knock knock

"*Mamae?* Is that you?"

I'm startled from my wet dream by my sweet girl's voice. "Yes, it's mama. I'll be out soon."

"Yay! Cuddles with mama!" She squeals and I can hear her trot away. I sigh hard and wash quickly, taking a moment to let the water beat my face. I needed to slap some sense into myself.

Wrecked

What was I doing? He's a sleazy biker who does business with my brother. He's another lackey under his thumb. No good can come from that. I sigh once more, a bit disappointed that I couldn't finish, but I had more important matters and that's quality time with my munchkin.

When I come out, she's fluffing up my pillows and propped up with the tv on, watching some show on animal planet. I crawl in beside her. She takes that moment to place her pillow in my lap and lay down, much like she used to do in Maua and on the ship. I stroke her hair as she soaks in the information about the Serengeti plains and their native animals. Although I'm staring at the tv, my mind has drifted off, imagining when I could get away from Frankie. I needed to increase the number of jobs I do to get more money since he's paying me pennies on the dollar. I'm thankful for Diesel's generosity when he gave me one of his shares. I misjudged him; not everyone who works for my brother is scum. But the majority are, so I have to keep my guard up. I don't have time for anything else.

Chapter Fifteen
Reaper

If I regularly messed with the club bunnies, Lil would be my number one draft pick. She made me forget all the bad things that happened these past couple of weeks. She reminded me she was only there to get off or to help me practice which still got her off. For her, it was a win-win. Our friendship hasn't suffered because of it and no feelings are involved. I still could not get Frankie's sister out of my head. I think Lil knew I was fantasizing about her when I would focus more on her than relieving my own pleasure.

I don't know why I can't shake these thoughts. She hated my guts, and it may seem mutual, but it wasn't. She caught me at my worst. When I was lashing out at the world.

I'm rattled out of my thoughts by the sounds of glass bottles clinking. It's old Josiah; you can hear him a mile away. As I said, Josiah was concocting the moonshine for the B.A.C.A after-party and bonfire. He drove this ancient Ford pickup truck loaded with old bottles he sanitized and filled with his potent brew. There is a bunch of digging equipment, too. He says it tastes better aged in darkness; that's why he has a maze of makeshift caves on his land. Anyway, since I hear his truck, I go outside to help with the cases of booze.

I see him in his signature overalls and tan thermal. "Hey Josiah, you need help?"

He shuffles over to the tailgate to let it down. "Don't ask stupid questions, boy. Course I need help. I'm 73 years old. I'm not young and full of muscle like you. Now come, put them muscles to work." He glances at me, "What happened to you? Looks like you've been dragged."

"Close, I was thrown off my bike and slid about a 100 feet or so. I'll be alright."

He shakes his head while I whistle for the fellas to help. He had four crates and six of those huge jugs. I wonder how he got them in the trunk. I don't think he's as fragile as he portrays.

Lucifer and Demon come out. "Josiah, right on time. Can't wait for next weekend. Here's the $500 for the brew and an added $100 for doing this for us." Josiah folds the bills and slips them into the overall front pocket. "Pleasure doing business with you boys. It's the talk of the town. Do you mind if I sell bottles in case they want to take some home?"

"You are welcome to do whatever makes you money. I'll grant you that request if you donate to B.A.C.A. before the night is done and the representatives go home."

Lucifer holds out his hand and Josiah shakes it, "Of course, this is a great thing you do for those kids, but I'll have you baying at the moon butt naked if you drink too much! This here is 120 proof."

I wince, thinking about the last time I had more than I should have. I woke up naked on the hood of Lucifer's truck. I felt a sting on my ass after Fiend used a fly swatter. I jumped up and chased him through the house. Or tried to...I made it halfway before last night's actions were forcing their way up my throat. I barely made it to the bathroom. I know my limits when it comes to moonshine.

We put the liquor in a dark corner of the garage per Josiah's recommendation.

"Well, I'll see y'all next weekend." We wave goodbye and head back into the house, each having tasks to complete before the event. Mine was food prep. We had a 15-quart deep freezer big enough to freeze a whole deer, but we weren't cooking anything exotic. It'll be the traditional BBQ spread. Fiend hops in the truck as we make our way to the grocery store. We both grab a cart for the massive amount of food we're going to buy. We may even have to make another trip this week if we don't grab everything. We start where every red-blooded American male would go, the meat section. We pick up packs of burgers, hot dogs, steaks, ribs, and every part of the pig and cow. Fiend's cart is almost entirely full as he makes his way to the condiments and I go to the dairy section. I grab blocks of American, Cheddar, Pepper Jack, and Mozzarella. I figure I should get chips to round out this trip. I entered the aisle and began grabbing bags when raised voices caught my attention.

Chapter Sixteen
Avi

It's been a long exhausting week working my ass off to save up, but it is so hard when I got so little. Every time Frankie bought something for Raven, he took it out of my next job. At this point, it was better to get her stuff on my own because what he was charging was outrageous. I decided to get snacks for the mini-fridge Diesel just put in my room. He said it was his, but he'd buy another one.

Because I couldn't drive and Diesel was on a run, I asked Frankie to have his driver take us, but he insisted on driving me instead. I have no idea why he wanted to, but I wasn't going to start an unnecessary fight over it.

I grab a cart from the front and push it through the store. Raven wanted to get in the cart, but I convinced her she was my big girl who could walk alongside mommy. She smiled as she grabbed onto the cart and walked beside me.

"What do you want first, munchkin?"

"Chocolate!" I chuckle, but I hear Frankie grumble. Always so damn serious.

"What?"

"Do you give her whatever she wants? How is she supposed to know it takes hard work to get the things she needs?"

"She's five, for Christ's sake! Besides, she's suffered enough, not that YOU would know anything about what she's gone through. Let me raise my child, okay? I'm sure you have some business to attend to; why are you here?" We stroll past the organic aisle and I grab some fruit bars. In produce, I pick up a bunch of bananas and have her pick two apples. She chooses one granny smith and one pink lady.

Frankie whisper yells as I try to shop, "Don't pin your poor choices on me, Avi! I made it out and look at how I'm living. Filthy rich and owning my own businesses."

I snort as I direct her to grab a loaf of wheat bread. "Ha! You sell poison to people, you literally deal in death, and if someone owes you money, I'm sure you've made them disappear. You're a two-bit criminal. And if you hadn't promised me you'd send for me right before you left me there, then I wouldn't blame you for my suffering. I waited day after day, month after month! After *mamae* and *papai* died, I was truly by myself and you didn't care!" We both looked around after I screamed at him. Raven looked at me, worried. "Hey, munchkin, grab your favorite chips for me, okay?" She nods and walks around the corner. I stop the cart and stare at him, "Why are you here? Your driver would have worked just fine."

"I needed to talk to you. Plain and simple, you're going to work in the club starting tonight. There's no argument about this, especially not here."

"I told you I would not work in your filthy little sex club. End of discussion." I started to walk away but felt his hand wrap around my arm and squeeze hard as he yanked me back to him. He was breathing hard and there was anger radiating from his body. "You don't have a choice, Avi and do you know why? Because I'll call child protective services and have Raven taken from you. How would it look? A single, illegal alien mom with no job, no income, and no drive. You're another burden on the overworked system and they don't take lightly to neglectful mothers. You could end up in jail."

My eyes went wide in disbelief. I couldn't believe the bullshit spilling from his lips. "You would blackmail me by threatening to take away my child? You filthy fucking bastard! I'm your goddamned sister! Not that whore you carry around on your arm."

"Daisy's not making the money she used to; she's too used up. She's been run through by every male in this town and plenty of passersby. It's time for some fresh meat. I know you need to provide for your daughter. You don't even have to start fucking; you can start with dances tonight and see how the men react, then I'll decide what type of girl you'll be. You can charge high-end prices and I'll only take half instead of 90%. See, I can be considerate." He smiled as if he had given me something for free when he was ripping out my heart and setting it ablaze.

I had angry tears running down my face; I couldn't even respond. Forced to do the one thing I vowed never to do again, give my body up for money. This was the lowest of the low, I thought I had fled the darkness, but here it was, disguised as my flesh and blood, in a cheap suit. He didn't care he was breaking my heart; he only cared about money.

"You start tonight. Daisy will help you learn the ropes or else..." He holds his phone up, dialing a number. I panic and grab for it, but he holds it out of my grasp, "Please, Frankie don't! She's all I have!"

"Then you'll do whatever I say?"

It's like the whole world stopped. I was standing under a big spotlight in utter darkness and he was in front of me, demanding an answer this second and forcing my hand.

"F-Fine."

"You'll do that and make runs for me. Now let's go; you're wasting my time." He shoves me forward and I feel so broken, but I have to get it together before Raven returns.

What was taking her so long?

I was horrified when I saw her peeking around the end cap. Her lip was quivering and tears began to run down her cheeks. Frankie didn't seem affected by her emotions, he stepped toward her and she stepped back.

"*Meu sol* let's go. Now!" He stepped forward and she stepped back again, shaking her head. "I won't ask you again, Raven Samara!" He raised his voice and I saw the same look when Maurice struck her. I can't believe I let her feel that level of fear again.

"You want to take me away from *mamae*!" She drops the bag of chips and takes off back around the other aisle. "Raven, come back! You bastard, what have you done?!" I scream as I leave the cart to chase after her.

Chapter Seventeen
Reaper

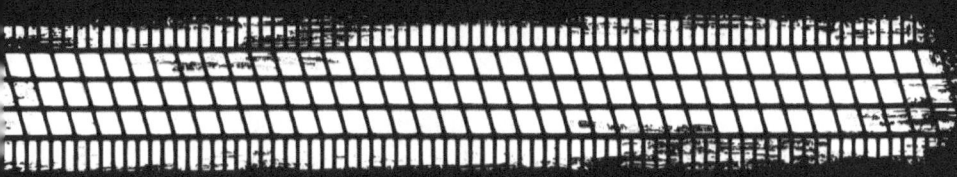

I'm looking for garlic onion pretzels when a precious little girl rounds the corner. She's in the cutest little outfit. I watch her looking tentatively at the endless variety of chips. An overwhelming selection of salty snacks for such a little one. I don't know why I'm intrigued, maybe because she's seemingly by herself, but she's confident in looking for her favorite snack.

She shakes her head as she sidesteps down the aisle, moving her finger up and down. I move back because now she's in front of me. "Oh..." She huffs as she cranes her head up. I clear my throat, "Do you need something up there?" Her mouth drops at the sight of me. I must look like a giant. She closes her mouth and nods. I understand she was probably taught not to talk to strangers, but I can help until her parents arrive.

I point to the pretzels and she shakes her head. Of course not, what kid wants dry-ass pretzels? I see some cheddar popcorn in a white bag covered with confetti, I point and she laughs this time and shakes her head. I squat down to her level. "Ok, tater tot, I know I'm a stranger, but you're going to have to tell me which chips you want, or I can lift you up there. Which one?" She ponders for a moment before she lifts her arms, signaling me to pick her up. She giggles as I position her in front of the top shelf selection. Somewhere nearby, I hear a heated conversation, voices raised then quickly hushed. She leans forward, grabs the sour cream and cheddar potato chips, and I set her down. She smiles so sweetly. *"Obrigado!"* (Thank you)

"De nada." (You're welcome) She gasped, surprised I knew what to say.

"Bye!" I wave to her as she turns the corner. Fiend joins me as we discuss what else to get during this run. Suddenly, I hear a raised male voice, then a little voice yelling before that same little girl runs around the corner, unmistakably upset.

"Watch the carts!" I shout.

I don't know where she's going, but it's dangerous. I chase after her as she makes her way toward the doors to who knows where. I lose visual as she passes the entrance to the outside, "Tater tot!" I wish I had known her name instead of the nickname I gave her. I look around and find her sitting cross-legged behind a bush across the street at the park. I slow down because I can hear her crying. When I get closer, I step on a twig startling her. She jumps and turns around. "Hey, hey, hey, it's me. My name is Cullen; what's yours?" Her big eyes were filled with tears. I hate to see a child in pain; it softens the most hardcore biker.

"Rav-raven."

"That's a beautiful name. I'm sure your mommy's worried about where you are. Will you come back with me?"

"No! *Meu tio* (my uncle) is trying to take me from *mamae!*"

"Who is your uncle?" That must have been the male voice I heard earlier and the ruckus. Her chest was heaving as she tried to calm down and remained silent.

"Well, we can't stay here."

Wrecked

"Raven! Raven, baby, where are you?!"

I hear a woman shouting; the panic in her voice is heartbreaking. She's frantically looking around for any sign of her child until she sees us. She races over and drops to her knees, hugging her.

"I'm so sorry, munchkin; you should have never heard those harsh words from your uncle. I won't let him take you from me." She squeezes her so tight like she would disappear and her daughter does the same. She stands with her daughter's hand in hers. She wipes away her tears, "Thank you for..." She stops when she sees me and I'm equally surprised. I didn't think she would have a child. But now I see the same beauty, the same beautiful deep-set eyes and sun-kissed complexion.

"You're her mother?"

Her facial expression changed quickly, "What's that supposed to mean? I'm incapable of being a mother since I'm a judgmental bitch?"

Well, no surprise she remembers me. This was another incident taken out of context. I didn't mean to make it sound like she was unfit; she seemed so young.

I was going to respond, but I saw Frankie marching this way. What the fuck did he want? Then I remember they're of relation. I silently pray to keep my cool with this innocent child around.

"Avi, let's go. I don't have time for this!" Her body language screamed she didn't want to go.

"Are you okay?" Those three words mean many different things, but I hope she understood what I was asking.

"Reaper! What now, are you trying to fuck my sister? Is this your revenge plot for taking your girl? We both know Daisy Mae looks much better on my arm, don't you think?"

She tried to cover her daughter's ears. "Frankie, language!"

I strolled up to Frankie, closing the gap as I glared down at him. My breath forced him to close his eyes every time I exhaled hard. I wanted to inflict the same amount of pain he seemed to be inflicting on them. Though it may not be physical abuse, some manipulation was happening. My senses are never wrong.

"This isn't about you picking up my leftovers and turning her into a crackwhore. You could never fill her like I did and she knew that. Especially at that little party you decided to throw at our clubhouse. After I left, who did she run to check up on, huh? Did she tell you she was going to the bathroom? Because she didn't."

I saw him get increasingly irritated after that revelation, "But we're not talking about Daisy. I'm making sure this precious little girl didn't get hurt running off like that. YOU should have been chasing her, not me, but you were the cause." I looked at Avi; now that I knew her name, it filled my thoughts except for the burning animosity I had towards Frankie.

"Is this how you treat your *familia*, Frankie?" I cross my arms and raise my brow.

"Don't you worry about how I treat *mi familia, seu filho da puta*! (my family, you son of a bitch) It's none of your concern, so back off!" He shoves me and before I go into a blind rage and beat his face in, I feel two small hands on my chest and look down to see Avi trying to keep me calm.

"Stop it, both of you! My child is here! She's heard and been through enough! Thank you for finding her, but we'll be okay. Frankie let's go. Come on, sweetie." She holds her hand out and Raven slowly approaches while observing me. I kneel down and tap her chin, "I'm okay. Take care of yourself and your mom, okay?"

"Okay, Cullen." She surprised me by hugging me. It was so innocent, so sweet.

"*Obrigado*, tater tot."

She giggles, "Bye-bye." I nod at Avi and they walk toward, no doubt, the only $75k luxury car in the parking lot. Frankie stares me down with no words until he's far enough away to safely turn around. I rub my face and groan loudly to vent my frustration. I got a bad feeling and again, my instincts are never wrong.

I walk back in to see Fiend in the same spot I left him. "Dude, what was that?"

"I'm still trying to figure out what happened, but that is Frankie's sister's daughter, Raven."

"The girl from the bar? She has a kid?"

"Yeah..." I push the cart, grabbing a few more bags of chips before we find a line to stand in.

"I don't know what that was, but you did not hesitate to chase after her."

"She could have gotten hurt; I wasn't going to sit here and watch."

"Uh huh..." I knew that tone. Here comes his unsolicited opinion.

"I'm sure she was appreciative that you kept her daughter safe. Look, you keep having these run-ins for a reason. Just... keep yourself open. That's all."

I looked back and he nodded and I knew he didn't want to elaborate. That was my job to do on my own.

Chapter Eighteen
Avi

Raven would not let me go once we got in the car. I carried her from the front door to our room and laid her down. The moment I let go, her eyes shot open. "Don't go, mama! I don't want to stay here anymore."

Same, munchkin, same.

I brush her hair out of her face. "I'm sorry for today, sweetheart. Mommy's doing everything she can so we can find a place of our own. I have to work tonight while you sleep."

"What if he sends me away?"

"He won't, sweetie. When I leave, you lock the door, then when I come back, I'll do our secret knock, so you know it's me and let me in. Will that be okay?" I know she wanted to say no, but she nodded. We used that knock almost religiously while I worked for Maurice. I wish it was something she never had to learn.

I made a quick trip to the kitchen to take some food into our room, so she won't be hungry while I'm degrading myself tonight. I grab some fruit and bags of chips. Then I make her a ham and cheese with mustard and a PB&J for later. I put everything in a canvas bag except the sandwiches. I slip into the pantry and grab some more snacks, filling it to the brim and top it off with bottled water and juice boxes. It was more than enough. I'm careful to tiptoe out and slip back in. She looked so relieved to see me and I lock the door behind me. I hand over the ham and cheese. She wiggles side to side while chewing happily and watching a popular cartoon show from back home. I busy myself by putting the food in the fridge and snacks in the lower drawer.

I was still in disbelief that he would blackmail me into working at the club, but part of me also thinks I should have known better. Money changes people. The sweet, caring brother who used to carry me on his shoulders up and down the beach while I flew a kite died long ago.

I set my alarm then stretch out across the bed and tell her I'm going to rest my eyes. I'll need to be alert for my night in Hell.

Chapter Nineteen
Reaper

The house phone rang while we were watching a movie. We pause it and wait for Lucifer to finish the call.

He paces while talking, "Yeah. When? What's the bounty? Uh-huh...and how many of us do you need? Wait, why? Yeah, because it doesn't make sense. What's your angle?"

You could hear him steadily growing angrier. "Yeah, well, that's not going to happen. We work for you, but this is MY family and my business, so fuck you, no thanks."

He slams down the phone, "Church, now!" Amidst his anger, he still kisses Sam's forehead, "Sorry, darlin'."

"It's fine. I'm going to bed...I'll be waiting to calm you down from whatever this is." She winks as she walks out of the living room. After ensuring all the girls are gone, we sit in the dining room.

We all sit around the table. "What's the deal, boss?" Demon asked as he paced the floor, grabbing his beard then he stopped and looked at me.

What did I do?

He clears his throat and rubs the back of his neck before he sighs loudly, "That was our old buddy Frankie. He wanted to contract us for a job."

"Okay, what's the problem, boss?" Wicked leans back against his chair, flipping his switchblade.

"The problem is he only wanted one of us...and that's you, Reaper. I smell a setup and I'm not going to let some arrogant, slimy bastard get a one-up on one of my boys."

Fiend put his hand on my shoulder. "It's because of that incident at the market earlier."

"What incident?"

"Nothing, that son-of-a-bitch was mistreating his family and I stepped in. I wasn't going to let him talk to her or her daughter that way."

Lucifer sits down, pulling a cigar from his vest with his cutter. Expertly cutting the head without so much as looking down. He inhales and the smoke billows out of his nose. "Tell me exactly what I missed because now our biggest contractor has a vendetta against you."

"Be real he's always had a vendetta against me and who the fuck cares?! I told you he's a fat, weasley piece of trash and today proved it."

"Aye, we were talking when a little girl ran past in tears."

"I helped her earlier with a bag of chips and then she went back around the corner to where her family was. Then there was shouting and she came running back around heading towards the door. All I thought about was her getting hit by a car, so I chased after her and found her crouched down behind a bush. She was scared he was going to take her away from her mother. Something wasn't right and I told him! He didn't care for that or the fact that Daisy ran after me the last time they were here."

"Well, that explains why he wants me to kick you out of the club."

"What?!" I almost blacked out in rage, knocking my chair over.

"Settle down; this is my club. What I say goes, not him. Besides, Sam would slice me from ear to ear if I allowed that to happen. This feud is getting out of hand."

"It's no fucking feud. I'd end Frankie with my bare hands. Nobody would miss him, not even his sister. She's not happy there, she said she was okay, but her eyes said differently."

All eyes fell on me and Fiend smiled, "I told you there was something there and now you want to be her hero."

"It's not like that. Besides, she can't stand me, but that doesn't mean I shouldn't help her."

I won't admit that my thoughts of her are borderline carnal. She had the most alluring eyes, even while she spewed obscenities at me. No matter how much she lashed out at me, I saw her soft side. She was beautiful and a nurturer to that cute little tater tot. I don't know why but I liked the nickname I gave her. She was energetic and had a smile that lit up the room. She was maybe no older than six. Her mother brought her here for a better life. Unfortunately, she had to rely on him to get it.

Then my phone rang, "Hello?"

"Reaper, it's Buddy. She's ready for you."

She's ready for you...

It echoed over and over in my head. A wave of anxiety washed over me.

"Reap, did you hear me?"

"Huh, yeah, I heard you. I'll pick her up in the morning."

I look back, "Betty girl is ready to come home."

"That's awesome, Reap! You get your girl back! If we are done with this Frankie bullshit, I say let's drink to celebrate! Who's with me?" Demon stands and everyone follows, even Lucifer. I raise my brow at him. "Hey, my boy is getting back on his favorite girl. I don't see a better excuse to have a drink or two."

"What about Sam?"

"Oh shit!" He growls and shifts his package, "We'll have a shot tomorrow when she gets here. Church dismissed!" He shot out of there so fast with the promise of satisfaction.

I felt the need myself but lost my fuck buddy to a relationship.

I was in the makeshift gym in the garage a few days ago when she sauntered in. I was on the bench press when I looked over to see a pair of legs in some very short shorts.

"Hey, can we talk?"

Yes, that sentence that makes every man shrivel up inside. I put the bar down and grab a towel as we wander outside.

She has her hands behind her back as we sit at the makeshift fire pit; it's where the bonfire will be for the event.

"You know we've been having fun and all; I've enjoyed teaching you the art of eating a girl until she taps out and I think you've become one of the best and I'm not blowing smoke up your ass..."

"What's his name?"

"What?"

"Come on, Lil. Men know when you say 'we need to talk', it's to break up and even though we're not in a relationship, the only answer is you met someone and it's getting serious. Now indulging in two dicks seems... wrong."

She bursts out laughing, "You got me. What gave it away?"

"Well, you blush across your cheeks when you're hiding gossip or when you're completely wasted and it's too early to drink."

"Okay, okay. His name is Everett."

"Jeez, Everett, really? That is the dorkiest name."

"Well, sorry, it's not cool like Cullen or Reaper, but I like it and him. Don't forget everything I taught you for that spicy siren."

"Lila..."

She holds her hands up, "Sorry! You still want to pretend, gotcha. But I know I'm right. Anyway, got to go; he's taking me to the state fair, isn't that cute?!" She squeals while swaying side to side. "Yeah, adorably wholesome. But for real, thank you for everything."

"No problem, don't go using my tricks on just anyone, especially that flick of the tongue on the... wow, flashbacks. I got to go. See ya later."

"See ya."

I shake my head to bring me back to the present. "Come on, guys, to the bar for the first set of shots of the night. To Reaper hopping back on and getting his boots in the breeze." I don't know why that caused me to rub my injured side, but the good news was the pain was minimal. I would have to see how bad the scarring would be.

Demon sets out the shot glasses and pours the Aberlour, a 12-year-old double cask whiskey. He lifts his glass, "To my brothers and what's to come!"

"Here here!"

Three shots later, "Fuck! I'm wired up and need someone to get into. Let's go to the Dollhouse. I need a toast in the champagne room if you get my drift." Demon nudges my shoulder.

After the third shot, I was feeling good. Why not celebrate with a lap dance?

Chapter Twenty

Avi

Frankie calls me to his office.

"What do you want?"

He slams his hands down while standing up, "Some goddamn respect from you! You live in my house and work for me, don't forget I can take it all away with a phone call. Got it?"

I roll my eyes. As much as he threatens me and radiates this anger to make me submit, it's an act. He's a puppy with a vicious dog attitude. All bark and no bite. Still, I can't take that risk that he'll make that call.

"You leave for the club in an hour with Daisy. She'll show you the ropes."

Great, lessons from the prized whore. "Let me work the bar, Frankie, please!"

"You will work the floor and stage; you're lucky I'm not putting you in the champagne rooms. If you get requested enough, you will. Lap dances are $100 and I take 60% of everything you make since you want to give so much lip. I'm giving you a two-week grace period for special services; after that, a blow job is a blow job."

I feel nauseous as he spouts it like I'm another girl he manipulated. I guess I was.

"If you start doing drugs, do that shit in private and don't let it mess with your performance."

"I'm not doing shit. I have a daughter! Is that all?" I couldn't wait to get out of his sight.

He waves his hand, nonchalantly dismissing me.

I storm out, slamming his door but straighten up when I see her coming towards me, probably going to screw him to stay in his good graces. It wouldn't be the first time; she shrieks so loudly that the whole house knows she's fucking the guy in charge. Little does she know I've seen a few girls in his office since I don't knock. I don't think he would give a shit if she did. He'd probably continue pushing the girl's head down his dick and look her dead in the eye as the girl choked down his load. I wonder why he kept her if he was going to sleep around.

She stops in front of me, a confident arrogance written across her face, "How the high and mighty have fallen, guess you'll be another slut like the rest of them." She laughs while looking down at me; funny how she didn't include herself.

I surprised her by stepping closer. I can smell the last ten guys on her. I see a hint of fear in her eyes; she should be.

"No, *cadela*,(bitch) the difference between you and me is that I am forced to work the club and give lap dances to ensure my daughter has everything she needs. On the other hand, you are so strung out that you'll do anything to get the money for the next hit, even give up your body. Don't you find it weird that your drug dealer boyfriend won't even supply you with a hit? No, he makes you suck dick and fuck for it...even with him. Shame. I'll be ready in 45 and waiting by the door. Oh, and I'd knock to make sure he doesn't have yet another girl under his desk like last time." I laugh as I leave her with that little revelation. Not sure how brain-damaged she is, but I hope it sunk in.

I get Raven ready for bed and we go over the rules while I am out. I make sure she has enough snacks and her new teddy bear I got her to cuddle up with. She named him Theodore. "Don't open this door for anyone. I will leave my phone and the phone number to where I am. Only call me if it is an emergency, okay?"

"Si, mamae." I kiss her forehead, tuck her in, and hand her the remote. "Sweet dreams...you too, Theodore." I placed a water bottle on the nightstand for her before grabbing my bag and walking out, locking the door then closing it, shaking it to make sure.

I say a silent prayer as I walk to the front door. Daisy was already there, dressed in a champagne-colored bandage dress that would look amazing on any woman, but she was so skinny it barely clung to her bones. She turns and heads out the door; the driver holds the SUV door open. I get in and am relieved to see Diesel in the passenger side seat.

He smiles, "What, you think I'd let you go in there alone?"

I smile and we are on our way. Lord, forgive me for what I have to do.

We arrive at the club; I notice it's not too far from the house. Diesel hops out and opens my door. I look at the venue and I feel my stomach drop.

"Hey, don't worry, I'll have my eyes on you the whole time. If you feel uncomfortable, call my name."

"Okay." I pull my bag tightly against me and walk in. In true trashy fashion, the place looked cheap and tacky. I follow Daisy toward the back and Diesel finds a seat at the bar.

The dressing room was small to have space for each girl. She drops her stuff at her station and points to an empty one in the corner. "That's your space. The shower only has cold water and sometimes the toilet backs up. The order of performances is tacked on the bulletin board; it looks like he added you to the rotation. You go on in...an hour. Enough time to walk around and get a few dances. Well, if the guys even notice you. I'm the top bitch and usually the one they want to see."

"You can suck them off like a brand new hoover, huh? I get the appeal. Glad you took my advice about covering your teeth." She was in such shock she couldn't even respond. She walked out to make her rounds, I guess. I didn't give a shit.

I sit and stare at myself in the mirror. What have you gotten yourself into, Avi? Is this any better than life in Maua? Yes... yes, it is, it has to be. You're earning money and your baby girl is at home in a nice comfortable bed sleeping peacefully. That's all that matters.

I try to stop my hands from shaking so I can put on my makeup. I change into a simple little black dress with side cutouts, pull and tease my hair into a high ponytail, and slip on my heels. Nervously, I walk out and head straight to the bar. Diesel handed me a shot; it smelled like cheap distilled vodka.

"Thanks." I take it back. It burns and numbs me simultaneously.

"I knew you'd need one. Most newbies do. Bartender, a second." I take the second as quickly as the first.

"You want to practice on me? I can always be your first." He waves a $100 bill with a smirk then he pulls out another $100. "I'm a good tipper. Besides, I know how much Frankie takes; consider the second a tip. Put that in your bra. So how about it?"

I snatch the two bills and he sat back against the stool. I finally pay attention to the music to find the beat to sway to. I stand in front of him and rock side to side, tracing my hands up my body and back down before rubbing my ass against his lap.

"Trying to cop a cheap feel? Won't I get you in trouble with your girl?"

"Nah, I told Emma where I would be and that I'd be your

first dance so you can feel comfortable. She knows you're like my little sister."

"I wish I was instead of Frankie's." I roll my hips and start to loosen up due to the two shots on a nearly empty stomach. I chuckle when I feel Diesel's little friend emerge and he scoots the barstool back to make space between us.

"Shit, Avi. You're going to make me have to jerk off in the bathroom." I can see the discomfort while shifting around his package.

"Go take care of it. My onstage debut is still 20 minutes away, that should give you enough time. I need another shot or seven."

"Alright, I'm going to facetime my girl. Don't forget to give your song selection to the DJ. Don't go anywhere with anybody, you hear me?" He slides past me in a hurry to relieve the boner I gave him. Isn't it weird he got one if he thinks of me like a sister? With the constant friction, he didn't have a chance. He was a man, after all.

"Bartender, long island iced tea shot, not the drink." It's much more concentrated than the cocktail. As he's making it, I consider what song I want for my first set. It shouldn't matter. I didn't want to be there but secretly wanted to knock Daisy off her high horse and become the most sought-after.

I decided to pick an American song I heard on the radio at the beaches or passing by the overpriced all-inclusive resorts. I couldn't help but dance to it and feel overly sexy. I needed all the help I could get to calm these nerves. The bartender sets my shot in front of me. "Thanks, put it on Diesel's tab." He nods before tending to the next customer.

I stopped by the DJ booth to give him my selection before standing backstage. "Hey, what do you call yourself?"

"Uhhh, call me *Lindo*."

In Portuguese, it means beautiful. I didn't want some

common stripper name like Candy, Lexi, or Cinnamon, or trashy, like Daisy. He jots it down and I wait for my cue.

"Alright, we have a brand-new doll in the dollhouse tonight and she's one sexy senorita. Let's give her a round of applause as she pops her cherry on the stage. Give it up for *Lindo*."

I count to 16 before I reveal myself to the hooting and hollering men. They haven't even seen me, but maybe because they announced me as fresh meat, they're excited to see new tits and ass. At least the alcohol has numbed my morale enough for me to walk out on the stage. I'm momentarily blinded by the light but not deaf to the whistles.

"Holy shit!"

"Man, what I wouldn't give for a night with her!"

Fat chance, buddy. I focus on the far wall to not actually look anyone in the eye, but I see the bills starting to pile up on the floor, so I grab the pole, dip it low in my dress, quickly flash them, and the room erupts. How they get so excited for so little. I walk around the pole teasing the hem of my dress, pulling it down to mid-thigh, flashing my bra, then pulling it up to show my cheeks peeking from the lace boy shorts I was wearing. I turn and face away as I bend over and tease them.

"Take it off! Come on, baby, show us all the goods!"

Malditos porcos... (goddamn pigs) Whatever, I am here to make money. I reach for the zipper in the back and slide the fabric down until it's on the floor and I'm in my lace two-piece set and heels. I drop to my knees and crawl around, the dollar bills sticking to my skin. I found the most innocent-looking guy for my target. His shaky hand held out a $10 bill. I think he expected me to take it and move on. He seemed so out of place. His buddies were loud and boisterous, the annoying ones who always cop a cheap feel. He was like the designated driver, so I decided I would make him the envy of his friends. I slid from the stage into his lap. I swear I felt a hiccup as he reacted to my warm body against him.

"Hi handsome, what's your name?"

"Fe-Felix."

"Nice to meet you, Felix. Do you know what *Lindo* means in Portuguese?" He shakes his head while I turn around and rock in his lap. "It means beautiful. Do you think I'm beautiful?"

"Oh, yes, yes, ma'am."

He's so innocent, so I turn back around and straddle him, getting close to his ear. "You were my first official lap dance and a perfect gentleman. Thank you for making me feel safe." I surprise him with a kiss on his cheek and his friends go wild while I hop off and finish my routine on stage.

I bow, "Give it up for *Lindo,* everyone. She'll be walking around waiting to give you the lap dance of your wildest fantasies."

I wish I didn't have to. I bowed once more as security started to pick up my earnings and put them in a bag. Then the spotlight turns off and once my eyes adjust I am face to face with the man of my wet dreams.

SHIT!

He looked just as shocked as I was. I felt the heat rise and settle into the butterflies in my stomach. Even from here, his commanding gaze made me feel like I was bare in front of him. It was then I realized I was still in my underwear. I couldn't get off that stage quick enough. I grab my dress and exit stage left, praying not to stumble in my stilettos.

What the fuck is he doing here?! Why tonight?! Who am I kidding? He could be in here every night. I plop down at my station; my heart is beating a hundred miles an hour. Why is he affecting me so much? I'm startled when a big burly guy comes in. "Here's your take. We automatically take Frankie's share, just in case you broads try to get slick."

"Yeah, thanks." As he hands me a handful of dollar bills. I took one of Frankie's security bags, tucked it in my shoes, and stuffed my socks in after. He stops before he steps out, "Oh and you have a lap dance request at table three."

"Me?"

"Yeah, asked for you specifically."

Great.

"Now!"

I jumped at his deep threatening voice. "Alright, *porra idiota...*" He still looked pissed, but I knew he didn't understand that I called him a dumb fuck. I put my dress back on, hike up my tits, and stroll past him. I walk towards Diesel and he pulls me into a comforting hug.

"You, okay?"

I force myself not to look over his shoulder. "With selling my body to men to survive? I think you know that answer. I want to get this night over with, so I can cuddle up with my baby girl."

"I'm sorry, Avi, sorry you have to do this. If it's any consolation you might knock Daisy off her high horse. She hasn't bagged a dance yet. All the other girls have been requested except her. She's been sulking in the corner."

"Apparently, I was requested, too. Where is table three? Some guy asked for a dance."

"Well, they have them numbered from back to front then across, so table one is the back booth by the door. That means table three would be the...oh, our Merciless Few buddies."

I squeeze my eyes close.

No, no, no, no, no...not them, anyone but them. Are you kidding me?!

"Lucky me. Well, I better get this degradation over with."

Wrecked

As soon as I sidestep around Diesel, his eyes are locked on me. He's sitting in the booth with his arms spread over it. Why do I suddenly feel a thousand degrees warmer?

No, Avi, you hate him. He's probably doing this to humiliate you. He called you a judgmental bitch.

But you ARE a judgmental bitch sometimes...

Thanks for the pep talk.

One of his brothers is getting a lap dance from a girl; I think her stage name is Bubbles. You know, bleach blonde, enormous tits. She's in a slinky gold number closer to a shirt than a dress. The other brother is busy with a set of twins in his lap. He definitely moved to the booth next door so the girls can comfortably molest him. I don't think they actually work here. Not when they're openly giving him a hand job. Then I realized I was staring at his dick.

I turned my eyes to the table; it was him and one other guy. I step up to the booth and lean forward with my hands on the table; it gives him a great view of my tits. I was going to say something sexy, I even practiced what I would say to my customers, but couldn't squeak out a word with his gaze on me. I see his lip curl into a smirk, knowing he caused me to freeze up.

His friend shifted to grab his beer. "Uhhh, so I paid for you to give my buddy here a lap dance since you two seem to run into each other everywhere."

His buddy is smiling like a jackal. He hands over the $100. "Is there somewhere private you can go?"

I lick my lips while maintaining eye contact. I see him trying to shift to a more comfortable position. "Sure, we have champagne rooms for special requests, but those are extra." They're not, but I should be paid extra for the humiliation. He pulls his wallet out and happily passes over $50. "Give him a good time; he's got it bad for you."

Then he smacks his buddy upside the head, the first reaction since I stood there. "Dude, what the fuck?"

"Come on, Reap... Lil even told me you called her name during sex. She said you turned into an animal when you did; now, here's the real deal."

They've definitely had a few before they got here.

I saw the sheer embarrassment on his face, then the anger. I hold my hand out before he kills his buddy for being a bit too honest. He looked shocked and surprised when my hand reached out for him.

"Come on, *querida...*" (darlin'). He stands up before placing his massive hand in mine. He shuffles around the booth to the opening and follows behind me. Diesel raises a brow and I shake my head. I see Daisy looking even angrier than usual from the corner of my eye. Then I remember when Frankie said he took Daisy from him. What a dick move, but honestly, he's better off without her. I glanced behind me to see his sights weren't exactly on where we were going. I turned around quickly so he wouldn't catch me, but I couldn't help but squeal internally.

I still wonder why we keep running into each other. Is he really fantasizing about me? Screaming my name out when he was with someone else. I can't help but feel a little jealous, then cynicism hit. Why would he want a stripper with a child? A drug runner and collector, *meu Deus,* (my God) I'm no better than my brother. And like that, my nerves set back in and when he sat down in the small room, I couldn't move toward him. He beckons me with two fingers. "Come." As much as that tone turned me on, I was still hesitant. He then chuckles to break the awkwardness while running his hand through his hair down to his beard. "I should apologize for what Fiend said. I'm definitely going to kill him later."

You didn't actually deny it, so it must be true.

"It's okay. I consider it a compliment. Didn't think I'd see you in a place like this."

"I usually don't frequent anything owned by your brother, but we're celebrating. I get my Betty girl back from the paint shop tomorrow. I'll be able to ride her again." He seemed really happy to relay that.

Seeing a softer side of him allowed me to move forward. The music playing through the speakers is loud enough to focus on. I straddle his lap and brush my fingertips against his scars. They're still pink, not fresh but not entirely healed. "What happened?" I felt him shudder underneath me.

"I crashed off Route 40 after I caught Daisy with her neighbor."

"Oh...I'm sorry."

"Yeah, everybody is...It doesn't matter anymore; she's with your brother."

"Yeah, he treats her like another notch in his belt. I mean, he makes her work here."

"Forget about her. Why are you here?"

"It's complicated...umm..."

"Reaper."

"Really, your club name?" Interesting, when he so quickly gave Raven his real name. Maybe because she was a child. Perhaps it's biker code cause that's how it is in Maua; either way, I'll respect it.

"Until the situation changes." Then he slid his hand up my leg to my hip. I almost lost focus because of the jolt of electricity pulsing from where he touched me. I 'm sure he felt the slight squeeze of my legs.

"I'm here because Frankie threatened to call protective services and have Raven taken from me if I don't. I can't risk it; she's all I have. I will do anything to make sure she has a normal life, even if I have to dance and work in the champagne room.

Even though I swore I wouldn't set foot in one of these, here I am with you. I guess it was inevitable; I'm just another whore to him, like Daisy."

His hand resting on my hip was now gripping it. "Don't say that! You are nothing like her." His raised voice made me shiver but also sparked my anger.

"What do you know?! On our first run-in, you called me a whore! You literally spat it to my face. Then you called me a judgmental bitch because I didn't want you to save me at the bar like I was some helpless little girl. Well, you're right! I don't want or need your help!" I shoot up and storm toward the door, but instead of opening it, I'm slammed against it by a huge biker guy mere inches from my face.

"Stop. Once again, you're taking things out of context, okay? I was wrong. I know you're not a whore or a bitch, you're trying to give that girl the American dream, but..."

I don't know why that dominating tone doused the anger but sparked a flame; now I'm panting. I want him to make the first move since he has already pinned me to the door. I wanted him to kiss me hard while ripping this tight piece of fabric off my body. I'm on fire as he holds his position, but I arch my back, closing the space a little. The silence is deafening and I can tell he is a hair away from wanting to bury himself in me.

bang bang bang

"Times up!"

I bit my lip hard, trying to will myself to resume breathing after he stepped back.

"Avi, you don't have to do this."

"Really, what are my other options right now?" I held out the $150, "Here, you didn't get what he paid for."

He steps closer, causing my body to hit the door again. He leans in and gives me a soft kiss, surprising me. The electricity had me pulsing between my legs so much that I thought I would cum right there. My knees buckled visibly. My body screamed for more...so much more.

"Keep it. I got more than what I paid for and here's my tip." As he pulls two $100 bills.

"I can't take this from you."

"I insist, put it towards caring for that little tater tot."

"That's twice you've called her tater tot."

He opens the door, "Yeah, she's cute when she blushes, like her mother. Take care, Avi."

I stand there for a few seconds trying to figure out what just happened. I slip the $300 into my bra and hand over the $100 to security waiting by the door. He handed me two twenties and walked off. My head was spinning and my heart was racing. I needed to sit in a quiet room and let it soak in, so I returned to the dressing room. A few of the girls were there talking about their clients. Apparently, they were very grabby tonight. I sit at my station with my head down after checking my watch, only a couple more hours.

Then I heard heels coming up behind me and stop. "What were you doing with my Cullen?" I heard her screeching behind me, but I didn't even acknowledge her by lifting my head. "Who?"

"Reaper, the biker from the club. He never comes to the club but tonight he shows up?! And then follows you to the back? What were you doing with him?"

I'm really not in the mood but decided to mess with her. I turn around, lick my lips, and smile while wiping the corners of my mouth, insinuating something dirty. "You know what they say, what happens in the champagne room stays in the champagne room. Besides, what business is it of yours? Surely if he wanted services from the 'top bitch' at the dollhouse, he would have come looking for you, right? Or he would've stayed..."

Pointing out he never would have dropped her cheating ass.

Her mouth fell open before she recovered, "Stay away from him! He is off-limits to the likes of you!"

"And why is that? Because you want him back? Is my brother not bottoming out like Reaper did? I saw the merchandise and he looked like he could fill me up just fine." It was a lie, kind of, I didn't see it, but I felt it. I'll have wet dreams about it.

Done with her cattiness and marking her so-called territory, I walk past her but keep my guard up; she isn't above a cheap shot.

Once I made my way out, I saw that the club had left and I felt mixed emotions, sad he left but glad he wouldn't continue to watch me demean myself. I found Diesel in the booth instead. "Where'd they go?"

"Home, I'm sure, especially Demon and his twin girl-friends. He's got a long night ahead of him. What happened there? He came out, said something to the group and they left. He did not look satisfied."

Well, we both weren't. More throbbing plagued me as my body begged for a much-needed release. I hope he didn't relieve his urges with that girl who he called my name. I didn't want to think about it.

"It's complicated. I got a few more hours, so I better make rounds before security tells him I'm slacking. See you in a few. He tips his beer at me and I take the time to speak to the customers and rack up six additional dances making a good amount with my tips to take home.

Chapter Twenty-One
Reaper

I wanted to hike her up against the door and, after she begged me, slide her down on my cock and take her breath away before she moaned my name. I wanted her nails digging into my skin, gasping at how I filled her up. She'd beg me to choke her harder while making her quiver around me. God, she'd feel so amazing when she came.

Fuck!

I left harder than I'd ever been in my life. So hard I was worried about jerking off. Once I rounded the corner from the so-called champagne room, I knew I had to get out of there. I couldn't watch her "work" in this filthy establishment. Forcing her hand to make a quick buck, Frankie was walking scum and I wanted to break both his legs. I also wanted to pummel Fiend for opening his big mouth and then have a word with Lil and her contribution in this.

Demon had already gone or was banging the twins in the men's bathroom or out back; either way, he wasn't in the booth.

"Let's go...now." I didn't give them a chance to argue. I had the keys to the truck and was already out the door. If I saw her before I left, I would carry her out caveman style to claim her and dare Frankie to step foot on our premises.

Fuck, I did have it bad. I needed to get myself together. Could I deal with a woman and a kid? A beautiful woman and a darling little girl. But an even better question is could I deal with her being Frankie's sister?

Chapter Twenty-Two
Avi

I did my secret knock and Raven answered so fast I'm almost sure she wasn't asleep. I kissed her cheek and closed the door, making sure it was locked.

"Back to bed. Did anyone come to the door?"

"Uncle Frankie did, but I said I wasn't supposed to open the door. He said if I needed food to press *22 on the phone and let Piedmont know. I said okay. Then I went to sleep. I missed you, *mamae*. When are we going to leave here?"

Good to know she had fallen asleep. I pulled out my earnings and placed them on the bed. Raven's eyes went wide when she saw all the bills. "You're a millionaire!"

I wish. I did rack up close to $700 tonight, more if you count what Frankie took. He's definitely going to make me work in the champagne room. I got less than two weeks to put together an escape plan. I put the money away, tuck her back in and go to shower and finish the raging inferno that beautiful towering Adonis started.

I hope my fingers can do the job tonight.

Chapter Twenty-Three

Reaper

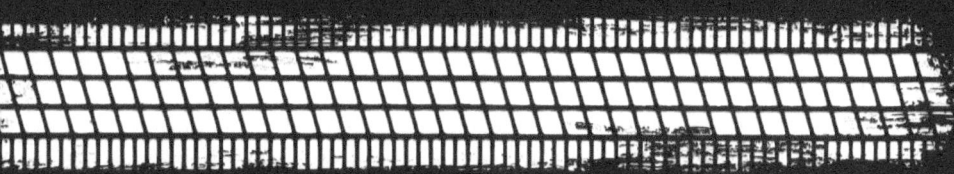

It's the day of the B.A.C.A rally and I get to ride my ol' lady. She was all shined up after they put her together. Her paint job was even better than before. Buddy even embossed 'Betty girl' on the fuel tank making her even sexier. I walked around her like she was a contestant in a beauty pageant, but there was no competition. She took my breath away. She groaned when I sat down, but she never felt better. I was still apprehensive until I revved her engine and basked in her powerful purr.

Instead of stopping at the end of the driveway, I made a right and was on the road like nothing ever happened. Exceeding the 50-mph speed limit because it felt right. The adrenaline was pumping as I approached the stretch of road where my life came to a painful halt. I revved hard and took the curve as smooth as butter. Throttling past that dark part of my life. I returned because the ride started and ended at our club-house. It was only 8 am and the ride started at noon. I placed her in her rightful spot in the garage with promises to see her soon.

I head into the kitchen for a quick bite. Sam and the girls

were prepping all the food for later, chopping the vegetables and making the patties for the burgers. She would ride behind her old man today, so she was in her crop jean top with our emblem and low rider jeans as she gave each girl specific directions.

I took that time to talk to my old buddy, Lila. Well, I grabbed an apple and took a generous bite. She felt my presence and looked behind to see me staring at her; then, she quickly turned back to slicing the tomatoes. "He-hey, buddy. How'd the ride go?"

"Great, she's like new and it felt good." Then I let the awkward silence torture her conscience.

She turns around, "I'm sorry!" I step back and raise my brow. "Now, why would you be sorry?"

"Don't bullshit me! Fiend told me he repeated what I told him. I shouldn't have said anything, but I wasn't wrong. For Christ's sake, it was like you were possessed but in a good way. I didn't know I liked to be choked until now. She's in for a damn good ride." She laughed and I felt uneasy having this conversation with the other girls around.

"That's not the point. Could you please refrain from any more details about our casual sexcapades?"

"What if she asks me?" She smiles wide.

"I'm not answering that question. You're going to do what you want anyway."

"Not if you don't want me to. I won't kiss and tell." Those words flash me back to the club when I felt the softness of her lips against mine. It was electric and then I realized that I was daydreaming and she caught on.

"Oh, something happened, didn't it?! Tell me!" She was jumping up and down like a kid hopped up on candy.

"I- I kissed her."

"And?!"

"And that's it. Frankie's got her working at the dollhouse; I couldn't stay and watch her work there."

"The dollhouse? Why is she working there?"

"She's got a kid, Lil. Plus, that bastard threatened to take her daughter away from her if she didn't. I knew I didn't like that heartless bastard, but now I want to wipe him off the Earth so she and her daughter can live in peace."

She punches my arm playfully, "Look at my little Reaper growing up and opening his heart."

I rolled my eyes, "I got to go get ready for the rally. Will I meet Everett at the after-party?" I rear back and smack her hard on the ass, enough for her to yelp and catch all the bunnies' attention. "Ow! Hands off the merchandise, I'm a taken woman now. And yes, you'll meet him tonight. Now go jerk off; your fantasizing gave you a major hard-on." She looks down, causing me to look, too. I wasn't showing, but she chuckled.

"Tease." She was right. I was going to fantasize about Avi's lips, those breasts, her smooth skin that smelled like honey, and her perfectly rounded ass. I bet her pussy was tight and wet.

I left quickly before I popped a boner in front of all of them. I close and lock the door to keep the curious bunnies out. It was her and me in my imagination.

Chapter Twenty-Four

Avi

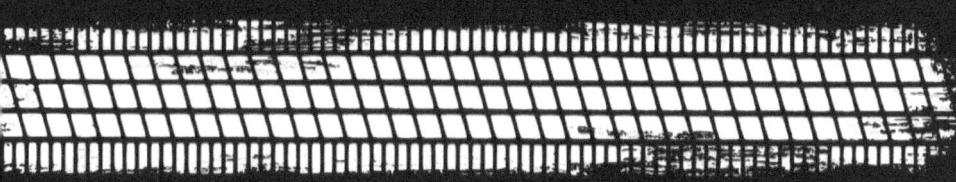

It was a quiet day and Frankie didn't want me to work tonight, which was odd. I have been bringing in more money since I started there. I'm a bit suspicious.

Raven is running around in the backyard, getting some fresh air, screaming and giggling. I oddly think about giving her another sibling, someone she could play with. One that would look very similar to a certain biker, but with my warm skin tone. I shake my head immediately; maybe a puppy is a more rational option.

"Mama, let's go to the aviary and feed the birds."

"Sure, take my hand."

After dinner, we were in our room when Frankie walked in. "You're coming with me tonight to the biker rally, be ready in an hour."

"Wait, why?"

"Do you always have to ask questions? Can't you do what I say?"

"Not when you take me away from my child."

"Can I go, mama?" Raven perked up, but it was definitely not a place for children.

"I have some business to settle with Reaper. I'm giving them an ultimatum, or I'll end our contract."

"What does that have to do with me? I barely know Cullen." I slipped up and looked over to see Raven perk up, "Ooh, Cullen, I know him! He helped me to get my favorite chips from way up high, mama. He's nice. I like him."

Me too, sweetie.

I see Frankie's face grow angry. He wanted to lash out and instill fear, but instead, walked out, slamming the door. Instinct tells me to do this to avoid animosity, so I find a thin, white long-sleeved shirt with a cutout in the back and some jean shorts. I curl my hair to put it into a ponytail with face-framing bangs. Raven comes in to watch me, "Can I go, mama?"

"Oh no, sweetie, this is a grown-up thing and there won't be any other kids."

"But I want to see Cullen again." She pokes her lip out and her eyes go all big. I don't know where she picked that up.

I put my curling iron down and pat my lap for her to hop into. I wrap my arms around her and she wraps hers around my neck.

"How about I tell him you said hello when I see him?"

"Yah, yah! But tell him that tater tot said hi. I like when he calls me that."

"That's twice you've called her tater tot."

He opens the door, "Yeah, she's cute when she blushes, like her mother...

I smile and nod, "Of course." She sits on the floor again while I finish getting ready. I keep my makeup light and simple, unlike when I go to the club. There I use my makeup to become a different person.

Soon there was a knock; it was Diesel. "Are you ready to go?"

"Thank God you're going. Do you know his deal?"

He shakes his head. I turn around, "Okay, go to bed and don't open the door except when I knock, got it?"

"Yes, mama."

As we head out, I get a bad feeling about the whole situation and didn't even know the entire story. We wait outside near the fountain in the center of the driveway. I enjoy the sound of the water, calming my restlessness.

"I don't like this. He's up to something, and somehow, I'm now a part of it."

"It's easy to see Reaper has never liked your brother and he's pretty open about it. He says Frankie would throw their club under the bus before he'd go to jail."

"I believe that 100%." He'd toss Diesel and me under there for good measure.

"The icing on this case of dynamite is that Frankie sought out Daisy while she was still with Reaper, about a week before his accident."

"He told me he found out about her and her neighbor. He didn't say anything about Frankie."

"I don't think he knew. I'm pretty sure he found out after one of his brothers saw her with him at the club. Well, she was blowing him under the table at the club."

Surprise surprise. Frankie was being vindictive.

I hear the front door open and Frankie walks out with Daisy on his arm. He's super affectionate and she's eating this crap up thinking he really cares. She's so obviously overdressed in a short red mini-dress.

"Let's go!" He bellows from the open door of the SUV.

"Let the three-ring circus begin, I guess." As we walk toward the SUV.

Chapter Twenty-Five
Reaper

This ride was exactly what I needed. The ride this morning was foreplay compared to this. I felt the familiarity of the breeze, forcing me to take deep breaths of cooled air. I throttled and opened her up, revving her like an animalistic mating call. Letting all eligible females know a man was present and this was my display of manhood.

But I wasn't deaf to the jokes of the other bikers about my noticeable scars; I got a ton of flack for that. I especially liked being asked if I needed a chaperone, training wheels, or if I wanted to ride in the back with the prospects. Those jackasses can joke all they want from behind my back as I rode proudly in front with my brothers. We wound through the countryside, getting peaks of lush green forests, mountains, and rivers.

The roar of the engines sounded primal as it warned any predators not to mess with such a large group. We totaled about 150-170 bikers behind us in a wide array of styles, from the classic Harleys to the more modern Kawasakis. Local townsmen whistled and waved as we rode by. Some of the back warmers flashed those same men while passing by. If I had an ol' lady, I'd never let her. Her tits were for my eyes only. With so many chapters, the locals are lucky to see this every few years as every location is thrown into a hat and the winner is drawn from the HQ chapter in Maryland.

Before we started the ride, each club President started the donation pot with $500 and every member would add in throughout the day and night until 8 p.m. when the B.A.C.A. reps were supposed to arrive. Our chapter decided to match our Prez's donation to a total of $2500 and the bunnies gathered up $500 between them.

Sometimes there's a negative stigma with club bunnies, but besides being sexual degenerates, they really had a big heart regarding kids, a couple being mothers themselves.

That's $3000 from our area alone. I hope we can hit double digits. I think the bunnies are supposed to hold a bikini car wash when we return to hose off our bikes. Hot girls in teeny weeny bikinis soaping up our bikes while they rub against them? Hell yeah, I'm in! I wonder if Everett would condone that. I'm expecting an accountant or a timid banker with a name like that.

The roars dull into a growl and then the hoots and hollers of the adrenaline rush. It's a mating call from the male bikers and their females responded, most couples celebrated with a kiss, some a bit more explicit than others, including ass grabs.

I wish I had someone to celebrate with. I wonder what her reaction would have been if I grabbed her by her tiny waist to pull her against me. Her hooded gaze as she moans to the feeling of my rock-hard erection as I run my fingers through her hair, tightening my grip before I dipped her into a deep kiss while keeping my other hand on her ass, slapping it when I set her upright. Grabbing a handful in her short shorts, marking my territory for all to see. She'd smile wickedly as we snuck off to christen my room, her screams ringing throughout the house.

Wrecked

I look down, I think it's time for my first shot of moonshine.

I go behind the outside bar where the moonshine was and set up the tap. "Drink at your own risk" was scribbled on a chalkboard next to the keg. I placed it right in front, a visual waiver that we are not responsible for actions after consuming the devil's nectar. I set up all the shot glasses we had next to the sign.

I pour a shot and turn to see the various activities starting. Lucifer was firing up the grill and Sam was bringing out the first tray of meat. The car wash was also in full effect, and by full effect I mean fully topless. This was not mentioned in the advertisement. I don't think they got into the moonshine, but they were in the kitchen earlier. Perhaps Johnny, Jack, or Jose made it into the rotation. Either way, they cranked up the music, lathered up their tits and suddenly there was a line to get your bike molested. The bikers were extra-giving, dropping bills into their tip bucket. I guarantee there'll be more tits on display by night's end.

I take that opportunity to take the shot back and I swear it lit up the nerve endings on my road rash...fuck! Josiah wasn't lying. It felt like pinpricks all over but lit on fire with gasoline. That was my first and last shot.

Well, now that I was about 100 degrees warmer, I removed my t-shirt before putting my cut back on. This was surely going to be an interesting night.

"Reaper!" I hear someone call me, it's Lila and...holy shit, that's Everett?! That fucker is massive, taller than me, like 6'6" at least; he looks like a corn-fed lumberjack. She looks like a child in comparison.

"Hey, Lil. This must be Everett. Nice to meet you."

His giant paw squeezed my hand a bit tighter with a smile. I knew that squeeze meant she's mine and I'm not fucking kidding; I'll pull your nutsack off where you stand.

"Likewise. I hope you know you can't get her back."

"Don't worry; she was a good pal helping her broken biker friend through a rough patch."

"Hey, you're not broken. You just won't admit it."

"Lil..." I scold.

She holds up her hands, "Fine! Baby let's take a shot, then go dance! What proof did Josiah make this time?"

"120, I shit you not."

"Fuck! Seriously? Ok, babe, only one shot, or I might let you fuck me in front of everyone on your bike."

We both looked at her; she wasn't kidding. I'm surprised he had a bike. He must be a part of a smaller group.

"What ya riding?"

"That all-black Triumph Street Scrambler over there by the barn doors. You know it's hard to find a decent bike if you're tall."

"Yeah, but that's a sweet choice. Respect."

Without thinking, I took a second shot and realized it would indeed be a wild night. My rash was super sensitive and responsive; even the breeze made me twitch.

"Oh shit!" Lil screeched. I thought she was reacting to the shot of pure petrol she threw down her throat. Then I saw her pointing behind me. "Umm, Reap, turn around."

I turn to see an all too familiar black SUV.

Chapter Twenty-Six

Avi

I'm glad I picked up some studded ankle boots when I could shop; it makes me fit in more, unlike Frankie and his bargain basement suit. You'd think he'd spring for a tailor to look less tacky. In fact, he and his suit drew unwanted attention and I felt uneasy. There were a slew of bikers, more than I expected, but this chapter was hosting the entire Northeast. There was a huge bonfire getting started and two giant grills going. They billow smoke and fill the air with meat-scented deliciousness. There was music blaring and tits on display. Apparently, it was their carwash.

"Come on, I need to find Lucifer and show him who's boss of this town. I own him and his fucking band of misfits. "

Ha!

I clamp my mouth shut and look at Diesel, who shakes his head at me. Frankie starts to walk around and I know I will run into him. I'm on his territory, and I knew I wouldn't fight whatever he had in mind by how he looked at me and took control. I was a sitting duck and what's funny is I looked forward to it.

Frankie finally finds who he's looking for, a gigantic mountain of a man with a silver beard. He had the same emblem Reaper did but slightly different, so he must be the head guy, or I think they call him the President. He sees us approaching and whispers something to the guy grilling next to him.

"Lucifer, I'm here to finish our discussion from our last phone conversation."

"Nothing to discuss. I ain't letting my boy go because you got a hard-on for him. If I remember correctly, you took his girl and you've been throwing it in his face ever since. I'm not sending him anywhere."

"Do you realize I hold your contract? Without me, you and your mangy pack have nothing!"

There goes my brother, more balls than brains behind enemy lines.

"And I don't think you realize where the fuck you are, Frankie. This is my house and these are my boys. If you have an agenda, that's not my problem. Reaper hasn't done anything except defend himself against your useless vendetta. To piece his life back together."

"I don't want that bastard involved in any of my business dealings or getting any cut of the money. I want him gone, or I'll find someone else to move my product!" He screams out, gathering the attention of the entire group. Judging by some of their looks, he was making a big mistake by being openly disrespectful.

Lucifer and the other guy set the grill hoods down. He looked familiar and then I realized he saw me dancing in the club. No, he paid for him to get a lap dance from me. I believe he recognized me as his lips turned upward when our eyes met. He almost looked like he was going to run and find him, like he couldn't wait to tell him I was here.

Lucifer stepped from behind the grill. "Oh really?" He turns his back, looking out to those gathered. "Attention, Merciless Few brethren, I want everyone to remember the face and name of Frankie Cabrera. He's here because he wants one of our brothers gone. A brother he wronged by stealing his girl and trying to get him alone to harm him. I will not allow my boys to be pawns in ridiculous fucking games. He wants to take our contract away, but I just ended our contract. Our brotherhood is unmatched. You mess with one, you have a problem with ALL of us. No one does business with him, hear hear?"

"Hear, hear!" They all yell in unison. It sounded like a crowd in a football stadium, echoing against the trees.

Frankie is irate and turning red as Lucifer turns back around and steps further into Frankie's space. Frankie pushes Daisy aside and puffs out his chest, but Lucifer chuckles. "Good luck finding some mangy bikers to run your shit. The entire Northeast is off limits and it's going to cost you a pretty penny for some private contractors."

Before another word was uttered, I saw the object of my desires approaching like a locomotive about to decimate Frankie, but Lucifer caught him, pushing him back, but he was as big and strong as his President. He may need a few more men to keep him away.

"Stop, Reaper, he ain't worth it!" Lucifer tries to keep the distance.

"I beg to fucking differ; I'll wipe this filthy scumbag off the face of this Earth. You're a parasite and how you treat your family is despicable!"

When he mentions family, his eyes go straight to me. I'm frozen in place and a blazing inferno at the same time.

"And I told you my family is none of your goddamn business! You want to fuck her to spite me. Well, you'll never get the chance! I promise you this will be the last time you see her, so you better take a long hard look. She's off-limits and so is Daisy."

Reaper gets by Lucifer and the entire party stops. I mean, it's whisper quiet for the setting of a giant celebration. Frankie was outnumbered, but his ego wouldn't stand down.

"Contrary to your belief, I don't give a shit about Daisy Mae, you can have her. You've turned her into your own personal coke whore and slut. Why would I want that back? Your sister, well... she's another story..." He smirked and I felt a million times warmer plus, he wasn't wearing a shirt, only his club vest. His pecs are surrounded by those minuscule pieces of leather fabric. I caught myself staring only to look up and meet his eye; he winked, knowing he saw me.

"What's the matter, scared another man can take better care of her than you? I guarantee she and that little girl won't be with you much longer. I'll give them everything they need."

Wow. Stunned couldn't even describe what I was feeling. I was wrong about him. I judged him in the heat of the moment. After our initial encounter, I thought he was some arrogant jackass, then I thought he had a savior complex when he rescued me from that brute at the bar. He didn't have a complex; he was protecting me. Making sure no harm would come to me. Doing the one thing I expected from my brother.

I let my abusive past get in the way. Maybe I don't deserve a guy like him, but here he was publicly laying claim and there's no doubt I want it.

"You'll never be a part of my family! I'll make sure of it."

My stomach dropped, could my brother actually kill me? He could send me back to the slums of Maua. I felt queasy; why was he trying so hard to hold onto me? He didn't want me in his house anyway, only if I was making him money.

I had enough saved for almost a year's worth of rent, but I had to factor in other expenses, too. It's nice to have a place but not if you can't furnish it or feed your kid. I needed to find stable employment, but I also had to be legal. I have a long road ahead of me. I was making progress toward my goal. I had to ease the tension between them before Frankie acted drastically against me.

I step between them, holding my arms out, facing Frankie, *"Irmão, por favor."* (brother, please) And next thing I knew, he shoved me to the ground, causing Reaper to sucker punch him. I didn't see it, but I heard it and saw Frankie hold his jaw while checking his mouth for blood.

"Don't you ever fucking touch her like that again!"

I wallowed in self-pity on the ground; I felt like less than nothing. I didn't even realize how close they were to fighting until I was in a cloud of dust because they were kicking it up, trying to scuffle. Diesel was holding Frankie back by the back of his oversized suit while Reaper was being held back by his entire brotherhood; I remembered all their faces from the club. Everything that Frankie put him through boiled over; putting his hands on me was the breaking point.

"You fucking coward, putting your hands on a woman, your own sister!"

Then Frankie does the unthinkable; he spits in his face, gets a cheap shot in, and it's an even bigger struggle to calm Reaper down.

They're going to kill each other!

"Cul-Cullen! *Por favor pare!* Stop it, please!" I turn around to see Raven, my Raven, running toward the commotion. What was she doing here?! How did she get here?! She's using her little legs to reach the men fighting, but I intercept.

"What are you doing here? Did you sneak into the car?!"

Tears are running down her face, "Stop them, mama! Stop them! Someone's gonna die! Please!"

Seeing her frantic and screaming doused all the flames from Cullen as he stepped back and ran his fingers through his hair. Raven broke free from me and ran to him. He immediately picks her up and she hugs him. All anger and rage seemed to disappear and his face softened.

I've never seen her so affectionate towards any male, not like this, and especially not with Frankie. He crouches down and places her on the ground, brushing her hair out of her face. "Tater tot, what are you doing here?"

She gave him a big smile. "Mama said they were coming to see you and I wanted to see you, too." He wipes her tears, "Well, hello, but you should go with your mama, okay? This is no place for princesses."

I looked around to see that the girls had covered up, the music was turned down, and everyone had put their drinks down or away. It's sweet and amusing that the fun had paused because of my daughter.

"Okay. But will you visit me?"

"You bet. Come on." He takes her hand and they walk toward me. I hold out my hand and she reluctantly takes it. She had formed a stronger bond with him than with her uncle. And judging by Frankie's face he was not happy about it.

"Hey..." He catches my attention. "I'm here." That's all he said before he pulled me into his chest. "555-4441, save it to your phone." He then kisses my forehead and for a split second I close my eyes and am in peace.

"That's it! Let's go! I'll make sure you regret your decision, all of you. Especially *you*." He points at Cullen.

He never took his eyes off me, despite Frankie's threat, and the heat radiated off him so much I felt it like a heatwave. I wanted him to kiss me like he dominated me at the club; I didn't care who would see. So, I did. I pulled him down by his vest and leaned up on my tiptoes to meet him. I longed to feel his big arms wrap around me and pull me against him, but time was of the essence. Every second Frankie witnessed would piss him off even more.

"Avi, Raven, now! Come on, Daisy Mae."

I exhale my frustration, but he tips my chin up, "Next time." I knew what he was implying more than the quick kiss and I couldn't stop the smile from forming. "I better go. Come on, munchkin. Say bye."

"*Obrigado!*"

"*Obrigado*, tater tot. Avi..." I swear he growled my name.

She giggled happily but I felt a looming catastrophe coming when we got home. Before tonight the tension was caused by Frankie not coming through with his promise of sending for me, but now I was 'sleeping with the enemy' per se without more than a kiss. To him, I am a traitor. I needed to protect Raven from whatever wrath I was about to endure. This would not go unpunished.

What was scary was how short the ride was from the club's house to Frankie's; guess I didn't notice before. I couldn't even come up with a plan. I did make mental notes on how to get back to the clubhouse, just in case.

"Mama, I want to see Cullen soon. Can we go back tomorrow?"

"You will never see him again! Do you understand me?! Not another peep from you, or I swear I'll..."

She cowered into me, burying herself. "Don't threaten my daughter! You don't have to worry about us much longer since we are such a burden, a reminder that you used to be a poor, useless excuse of a brother and son! I hope you know they would be ashamed of who you've become if they were still alive." Referring to our parents sent his rage skyrocketing.

When we stopped, I rushed Raven out and to our room. I knew he wasn't done with me, but I didn't know if he would lash out at her. I could handle whatever my brother would dish out.

"Stay here. You do not open this door!" She nods as I close

it. I don't even get to turn around before hands grab me by a fistful of my hair and drag me down to his side of the house, shouting obscenities in both languages. We turn down a dark corridor and into a door on the left. He swings me forward and I fall on my hands and knees.

I can't even take in my surroundings before he yanks at my hair again, forcing me to look up. "You want to be a whore for them? I'll make sure you get enough practice Avi..."

What did he mean?! I'm shaken when he straddles me, ripping my shirt open and exposing my bra.

And now...he's another sick predator.

"What are you doing, Frankie?! Get off me! I'm your sister!"

He laughed wildly while hovering over me, "After everything I gave you when you were fresh off the boat! I could have left you there to fend for scraps, but then I'd be the bad guy. Now you're screwing my enemy!" He was so close that he was showering me in his spit.

"I. Never. Fucked. Him!" I twist and turn to get him off me.

"But you want to. You were going to cum right there when he touched you. Oh no, if you're going to open your legs for anyone, it will be for a price. BECAUSE I OWN YOU, AVI! And you'll pay me what you owe, but first, since he's been so vocal and eyeing you like a piece of meat, he'll get to break you in. Diesel! She's all yours."

He said like this was a normal conversation while he rolled off of me, which relieved me that he wasn't going to do something unspeakable.

Diesel's demeanor didn't reflect the kindness he had shown me over these past weeks. He stepped forward, looming toward me, growling while fisting his hands. I was not getting enough oxygen to comprehend what was happening at this moment. I tried to calm down because who knows what would happen or be done to me if I passed out.

"Diesel..." I croaked as a plea not to do this, but he didn't respond. He remained stoic and determined. Maybe he lied to me. Maybe there was no girl in California waiting for him. He used that story to trick me into letting my guard down and I did.

I'm a fool.

"I said take her! Have your go before she's run through. Yeah, *irma*, you're going to be a platinum level escort..."

I feel my stomach churning hearing his vile comments. I realize that this could be a life-or-death situation. If I have to, I will walk out of here covered in their blood.

Then Diesel turns around, getting between Frankie and me. "No."

Frankie chuckles, "No?! What the fuck you mean, no?" He couldn't believe that he would blatantly defy him. I've never been so relieved in my life.

"I said no. You've gone too far and why? Because you got a vendetta for a biker whose girl you purposefully stole. No one really even knows why you decided to do that. One day you suddenly had a problem with him. Then you turned her into a prostitute to make you a little money and she stays because you support her habit, isn't that right? But not for free, or because you care or anything. But because it's always about business, isn't it? And you would do the same to your sister? Your sister! She came here looking for better, looking for you to help her. She's right; your parents would be ashamed of their son. A money-crazed coward!"

Frankie looks back and then at us with his hand on his hip, "So, you've formed this little protective bond with her, too, huh? Is everyone batshit crazy over you? You make the men around here act stupid! This is MY empire and I won't have you come in and wreck it! This is why I knew I wouldn't send for you or anyone; it was only supposed to be about me! I worked for a man who wouldn't spit on me if I was on fire, but I leveled up and he became so impressed he made me his understudy. Two years toiling under him, learning the business and detailing all his mistakes and what I would do differently. He said I'd have as much success as he does and that night I did, when I put a bullet in his head while he slept. Always keep your guard up!" He taps his temple.

"I took his property, his ships, his inventory. It all became mine! Never trust anyone and that means anyone! I should have known when you always wanted to escort them to the club, or you'd follow her around the house like a love-sick puppy. I knew she was trouble."

"You mean when I was protecting her and her daughter like a man is supposed to? You weren't going to send for your own flesh and blood?! I couldn't even fathom that. Unlike you, I want to see Avi raise her daughter without having to demean herself or sell her body. Would you force your niece to do the same?"

Frankie steps back as if reality hit him and knocked the wind out of him. Diesel looked at me, relieved that maybe what he was saying was sinking in.

"Hmmm...a mother-daughter duo would really draw the men in..."

WHAT?!

Both our mouths fell open in utter shock; Satanas (Satan) himself stood in front of me cloaked in the skin of *minha família. (my family)*

He looks at us while rubbing his chin, "Relax, Avi would be too used up by then, but that was a pretty good idea. I'm impressed." He chuckled while pointing at Diesel.

I don't even remember lunging forward, but I realize Diesel is holding me back. "You sick fuck! I'll kill you with my bare hands before I let you or any pervert fucking touch her!"

Wrecked

"And I'd let her." Diesel said while keeping me away.

Frankie was so quick with his movement I couldn't react until after the gunshots rang out. I screamed and crumpled to the ground. I didn't even give myself time to assess.

Was I shot?

I didn't feel pain. I slowly uncurl my body, seeing no blood and feeling no pain.

Nothing, just uncontrollable shaking...and then I realize...

Oh no.

Chapter Twenty-Seven
Reaper

The whole group held me back as he slithered away with a frightened woman and child.

" My crew! In the house, NOW!" Lucifer shouted, then he turned to the crowd. "Continue the festivities." And like a record, the needle touched the vinyl and everyone was back into party mode, but I was heated as they shoved me through the door of the house.

I vent my frustration by slamming my fist into the nearest wall. Followed by reacting to the feeling of crushing your hand into plywood.

"Fuck! I know that son of a bitch is going to do something to her, I know it and it's because of me."

Lucifer stops my pacing by stepping in my path. "Shit, I've never seen you lash out. Not even with that dick-jumping harpy. In all seriousness, you need to calm down. We'll find a way, alright?" I hear that fatherly tone and he's right; I can't think straight. I'm going to kill him and I'm going to enjoy it.

"No! I can't think about anything but her and that little girl. This is crazy! How does this even happen?"

I plopped down on the couch, contemplating what I could do, no, what I WILL do. I wanted to ride over, bust down the door and carry them to safety as the house burned down with that bastard in it. Well, I guess I'd need the truck for that; this wasn't an action film, and I also didn't want to do prison time. Though I was contemplating how true that statement was. I wouldn't want to be away from them, but for their safety, it is a possibility. My thoughts are all over the place.

Lucifer glanced at the clock, "Look, the B.A.C.A. reps will be here any minute. Let me take care of our obligation then we can figure out what to do next. Someone call Sam for me."

Fiend whistles and calls Sam from wherever she was. She smiles when she sees her old man but frowns when she sees the gaping hole in the wall next to him and the raw cuts on my bleeding hand. I kept opening and closing my hand trying to dull the throbbing but I'm sure it only assisted the bleeding.

She shakes her head, probably disappointed in me, and grabs the first aid kit while talking to Lucifer, "Darling, the reps are here. The total raised is $18k, okay?" She kisses him while he grabs her ass. "Go, let me take care of my boy."

He kissed her forehead, which reminds me of when I kissed Avi. Now I'm more worried about her current status. She couldn't stay there another minute; every moment there was a chance for him to hurt her or worse. I didn't even realize Sam was cleaning my hand until I felt the sting then burn of the alcohol and I hiss.

She had concern written on her face. Everyone had gone back outside, but I couldn't do that. I couldn't go to sleep or anything.

"Earth to my big-hearted son."

"Huh?"

"So that's the girl Lila was referring to, huh? She's pretty, a real spitfire, I can tell."

Does everyone know?! Whatever attraction we have must leave a glow for everyone to see except for the people involved.

"How much do you know?"

She chuckles as she unrolls the bandage. "Listen, I could know nothing about her and see from how you touched her, looked at her, and defended her that you really care. This is the Cullen I know, the big heart who needs a girl like that."

"You don't even know her."

"I know what I saw. Now that your hand's all wrapped up, stay here, and after the presentation, you guys can figure something out. Don't you even think of going off by yourself, either! Frankie may act macho, but that coward will cheat anyway he can and I don't want you hurt! Do you hear me?!" Her voice cracked a little, which brought me back to my senses.

I take a deep breath, "I'm sorry..."

"Don't be. Any girl would be lucky to have a man to care for and protect her like that. You've healed from the accident and awful breakup to overcoming your fear of getting on your bike again. Now you'll get the girl and that precious darling. Tell me, are you ready for that? It's a big responsibility."

I knew she was referring to Raven. That little girl made me think about what I wanted in life. This brotherhood had been my family since I left home in South Dakota. I wandered my way east and ended up here eventually. My parents were the perfect couple, married 32 years and counting. I always ring them on their birthdays and anniversary and they always relay how much they love and miss me. They're great and were always so supportive. I want to be that support for Avi and Raven.

"She's my tater tot." The first time I said what I was thinking out loud. I can take care of her, take her to school, help raise her and watch her grow.

Then suddenly, I hear a weird sound coming from the

outside that seems to be getting closer. Then, bursting through comes my little lady. She frantically looks around before spotting me, then she uses the last bit of energy to run and collapse into my arms.

How far had she run? Frankie doesn't live far but for someone so tiny, it's a trek.

She's breathing hard; her face is dirty and tear stained. I don't want to go nuclear, but I swear I see the imprint of a hand on her face. If he put his hands on her, I'll make sure he has a closed casket funeral.

Sam looked as shocked as I was. "Oh my god, she must have run from Frankie's house, but he's at least a mile away! Poor baby, let me get some water and a blanket."

I couldn't contemplate what was happening right now except that this little girl was in distress and came to me. She felt safe with me.

"Raven, tell me what happened. Try for me, sweetie."

She started bawling while wiping her nose. "I-I-I he-heard... gunshots. Uncle Frankie, he hurt her...he hurt me, look." She said as she pointed to the large handprint.

I fucking knew it.

"Where is your mom?" I look at the clock on the wall and realize it's been a little over an hour. But enough time for Frankie to obviously have done something to her. If Raven heard gunshots... I shook my thoughts of dread, but I needed to get to Avi. Time was running out.

Sam comes back with the water and drapes a knit blanket over her because it was a chilly night and she was shaking. "Here sweetheart, drink some water so you can tell us what happened."

She took a few sips and then was panting as she tried to tell us what she knew. "*Mamae* is in trouble! He put her in the big car. I don't know where he took her. Please, find my mama!" Her eyes fill with unshed tears pulling at my heartstrings.

"Of course, sweetie. I will bring her home and you two will stay with me. I mean, if that's ok with you, Sam?"

She pats my hand. "You never have to ask. I'd love to have them around. We can... make some pancakes if you're hungry. How does that sound, darlin'?" Sam uses her soothing, calming motherly tone so Raven would warm up to her.

"I like pancakes, sometimes with nanas or choco chips!" That seemed to cheer her up but only for a moment, then she hiccupped and her face fell. She was terrified for her mom.

So was I.

"Well, I think you're in luck; I have both. Come on, let's whip some up. Maybe the big biker guys outside will want some."

"O-okay."

Sam leans over; she's fighting back the tears. "I can't imagine what this poor girl has gone through. I'll watch her while you figure it out. She's so precious; I'm already in love."

I know Raven's in good hands and in the safety of over 100 bikers who would kill anyone who harmed a child in any way.

I'm relieved to see that Sam understands, but now the part of me that had calmed down was burning uncontrollably. I have never let my anger get this out of hand and I fear what I might do in a black-out rage.

Wait, no the fuck I don't.

Chapter Twenty-Eight
Avi

I didn't want to look over. If I wasn't hit or hurt, I knew what happened. Those bullets went somewhere. I can hear my heartbeat simultaneously with the ringing in my ears when I come face to face with the umpteenth dead body in my life, but it's so much more heartbreaking when you're fond of that person.

He was supposed to leave. To set himself free of my brother. To be with his girl in California and live happily ever after.

This is my fault.

He's dead because of me!

"Diesel!" He was face down and I rolled him over to see the three gunshot wounds riddling his torso. I looked up and, to my surprise, he was looking back at me. He was still alive! He reached out for me while his other hand covered the wound near his heart. There was no fear in his eyes, like he was trying to keep me calm even though he was critically wounded.

"Oh, Herschel. I'm sorry, I'm so sorry! This is my fault!" I squeezed his hand so tight as the tears soaked my face and his shirt.

He sputtered and blood tickled out the corner of his mouth when he coughed, but he managed a small smile, "No. Worth it, take care...of her."

"Don't talk. You can make it! We can still call 9-1-..."

bang

I screamed so loud that it echoed through the room. When I looked back, his chest had a gaping wound and he was no longer moving. As fast as I could, I scrambled away from the body and wherever Frankie was. My vision hadn't cleared from me squeezing my eyes so tight.

I wanted to open my eyes to happier times when Diesel would spin Raven around until they were both dizzy. He'd pretend to fall and she would tickle him until he 'tapped out'. Of course, he let her win. He loved to see the joy on her face.

I realized something devastating; I was wrong. Not only had she opened up to Cullen but to Herschel as well. He loved my daughter, too and now... he was dead.

I didn't hide my absolute utter disgust. "You should be dead, not him, you son of a bitch!" I stormed toward him until he raised his gun and I froze. I hear him cock it, ready to fire. He kept his aim as he stepped toward me.

"I'm your family, me! I saved you, gave you work, fed you, and allowed you to board here rent-free!"

I was so sick of money being his priority instead of his *maldita familia* (goddamn family). I step forward until the barrel is pressed against my chest. I can see the shock in his eyes. I was calling his bluff, but there was a greater chance he'd pull the trigger without a second thought about Raven. He'd probably throw her in an orphanage.

"Don't you dare ever call yourself my fucking family when all I was is cheap labor. Everything is about money with you! What about love and support? The people who loved you when you didn't have a single *centavo* (cent)! No, all we are is a burden! And I need to get out of YOUR house, so you don't have to worry about me. What does it matter if I like Cullen or if he likes me? Why would he want anything to do with Frankie's sister? Are you happy, or would you finally like to end your awful goddamned suffering?!"

I was so sick of his shit; if he told me to get out and never return, I'd do it with a smile.

"Don't fucking tempt me, Avi. I still own you and you're going to work the champagne room tonight. Now go! The car is waiting."

He didn't even acknowledge what I said about family. He was too much of a spineless coward to face the truth.

"Now?! I have to check on Raven first and I'm covered in blood! Diesel is dead! What is wrong with you?!"

"Nothing, I'm all about my money, remember? Piedmont can make sure she stays in her room. We're going NOW! GO!" He points the gun towards the door before returning it back to me. I walk but watch as the gun follows my movement. I was putting nothing past him. I pass the threshold and he's suddenly behind me with the gun in my back.

"Let me check on her. I'm begging you!"

"She's fine. I'm sure you have enough food hoarded in there for her to stay alive until you return. Now go! I'm going to make sure even Reaper won't want you. And the next time I get him alone, I'll gut him from ear to ear."

His confession stopped me in my tracks. Irritated, he shoved me hard enough to fall forward to the ground.

"Mama! Mama!"

I'm horrified to see Raven and to know she witnessed her uncle pushing her mother.

"Don't push her! You're a bad uncle! I hate you! I want to leave here mama!"

"Raven, baby, go back in the room. Mommy has to work. I'll be back later."

"No, mama, stay here! Don't leave me here alone. I don't like him. I want Diesel! I want to go stay with Cullen!"

Oh no. Before I could get up to protect her, Frankie stepped past me, reared back, and struck her.

THAT FUCKING MONSTER HIT MY DAUGHTER!

Raven screams as she falls down, covering her face where he hit her, and starts bawling.

"YOU'LL NEVER LEAVE HERE! Diesel is dead and Reaper will be, too. There'll be no one to want you, you little brat! Piedmont, lock her in her room!"

Frankie turns to me and pulls me up by my hair and I start to wail on him. I got one arm free to reciprocate what he gave my child. I put all my anger into it, but he chuckles while wiping his mouth, checking for blood.

"If you weren't making me money, I'd end your pathetic life right now and toss your body in the ocean. I don't need you, her, or anybody! Final warning, do what I say, or I'll kill her right in front of you; then I'll keep you alive while you replay her death over and over. Is that what you want?"

I shook my head furiously. I couldn't fathom a moment without my precious baby girl. I had to do whatever Frankie wanted to keep her alive. How was I going to get us out?

Piedmont approaches and seems unbothered by the scene in front of him. "Take the brat and lock her up in the room. We're going out for the night."

"Yes, sir." He gently helps Raven up and she looks at me with so much fear but no tears. No, she had witnessed too much; now, she was numb in shock.

What was another traumatic moment?

Once again, mommy let you down.

"G-go, baby, mommy will be back, okay?"

"*Mamae*...." Piedmont is gentle with her and walks her down to our room.

"There, she's safe. Daisy Mae! Let's go!" I hear her heels clicking as I finally reach my feet. There were so many emotions that I knew I was on a hair-trigger and didn't want to hear any bullshit from crack house barbie.

Frankie had put the gun away, but it was still there as a reminder that he could and would blow me away. I walk outside and into the car. This was my lowest and all I wanted was a grand heroic gesture from a man who probably doesn't want to deal with a headache like me.

I slink into the SUV. Help me, Cullen...

Chapter Twenty-Nine
Reaper

Sam and Raven were making mini pancakes for whoever wanted any, but also sampling them. They had three different batters going: blueberry, chocolate chip, and banana. I could hear her squealing and laughing with Sam. She brought me a small plate of some she made personally. I smiled and took it from her, but I was too angry to eat. I set the plate down, pacing the room with no solid plan coming to mind. I wanted violence, I choose violence, but I knew that wasn't right if I wanted to be in her life.

The door startles me as it opens and it's my brothers.

Demon and Fiend sit down noticing my plate, "Sweet, pancakes! You don't want any?" I shake my head and they both grab a couple from my plate.

Lucifer steps up to me, "You okay, son?"

I shake my head, "Take a look, the situation just got even more complicated." He walks behind the sofa while the rest crane their heads to see Sam and Raven singing and dancing to the radio.

"Is that Frankie's niece?! How'd the hell she get here?"

I pull at my hair to keep myself from groaning loudly, venting my utter frustration at it all. "She ran here..."

"She what?!" It was almost like a group chant. The shock on their faces mimicked mine when she ran in. But as quickly as they were shocked, they had to straighten up when she walked in with Sam. She held the extra plates while Sam set down the variety platter.

"Guys, you remember Raven. She's helping me make pancakes for the bikers and you get first dibs because she said she liked you guys most."

The guys grab their plates. "Well, thank you, sweetie. My guys and I appreciate the nice words and yummy pancakes." Lucifer answers for the group.

She giggles as she hides behind Sam's leg. "Come on, tater tot." Sam holds her hand out and she happily takes it.

"How'd you know?!"

"A little birdie told me." Then she points to me. Then she does the sweetest thing; she waves before they return to the kitchen.

My face falls after putting on a smile for her.

"Reaper, how the hell did she get here?"

"She ran from Frankie's, something bad happened after they left here. She said she snuck out the window after Piedmont, his butler, locked her in her room."

Fiend checks to see if they can hear us whisper yelling. It's a loud, aggressive whisper. "Well, where's her mom?"

The rage crept up again, knowing I had to mention him again. "That bastard Frankie took her somewhere, but she doesn't know where."

Lucifer lights up a cigar, but stands in the doorway, "Frankie owns a few drug houses and the strip club. You said he had her working at the club. He's probably forcing her to work as punishment. Not going to sugarcoat it he's probably going to force her to solicit. Let's arm up. I don't put anything past that slimy bastard." Him giving us the go-ahead to strap up meant this would turn into a bloodbath.

At least, that was my goal.

"I didn't tell you the worst part; Raven came in with a large handprint on her face." The look of disgust said it all, "Now you know why I want to stomp his brains into the ground."

We all head down to the basement, where we keep everything. I'm going to get her mother back.

Chapter Thirty
Avi

"You dance first before you go to the champagne room. I want a $1000 minimum from you tonight; 100% goes to me. After the dance, I want you back there sucking dick immediately! Daisy, congrats; you got the night off from getting on your knees but get a few lap dances anyway. I might give you a bump for a good job." A sly smirk flashed across her lips; she was reveling in my downfall. He was going to make me no better than her.

If Cullen found out, I would be absolutely ashamed. Why would he want me after this? I'd be another dirty whore, a club rat, a bar skank.

I think back to when I called him a mangy biker, but he wasn't. I said it out of anger. They were all so protective of each other, like a family.

As I put on what they call a dress, I wonder what I want my ultimate ending to be. Would it be me and Raven living in our own space? Would Cullen be there? We'd have that time to get to know each other more. He and Raven would become inseparable. Could he be that father figure I always wanted her to have? Could he be that man who would love me past my flaws, past all this? I shook my head because my fantasy would never happen, thanks to my brother. I'll be in his servitude forever.

I make my way to the stage, but Frankie intercepts, talking but not looking directly at me, "Don't half-ass it, Avi and I mean it. How much does your daughter's life really mean to you? At least you'll finally get the attention you've been dying for."

What does that mean?!

No time to ponder. I had to power through this degradation. My mind wanders, I pray my little one is safe. As long as I can see Frankie, I know she's safe. But I also miss Diesel terribly. He made me feel safe at the club, now I had no one.

As the DJ introduces me, I close my eyes and take a deep breath. "Welcome back to the main stage, the lovely *Lindo*. We know you've missed her pretty face, so show her some extra love. She'll take clients in the champagne room after her set and a 30-minute break."

At least I get a break before I demean myself further. I take to the stage and the bills fly. The men hoot and holler; it's loud and obnoxious.

"Oh *Lindo,* I can't wait for my turn in the champagne room."

His buddy nudges him, "We all can't wait! Maybe she can double-team us? Would you like that, baby girl?"

I wish that sweet young man was here to keep me hopeful that the world isn't full of a bunch of garbage-munching pigs, but he was nowhere to be found. He was probably at home studying for his finals or midterms. Making a better life for himself.

That's what I was supposed to do.

I'm on autopilot wanting this nightmare to end. They don't care; it's tits and ass on display with a guaranteed happy ending via the DJ's announcement. They still litter the stage with bills.

Since I have a minimum to make, I can try to make a good

chunk now. The more I make here the less I have to do behind closed doors. I walk forward and squat down at the end of the stage and one brave guy comes close. "Holy shit, you're so damn beautiful." He's staring between my legs and I tip his chin up. "I'm up here. You want more; you'll have to show me you want it. Do you want it?" I lean forward to end up on my knees in front of him, squeezing my breasts. I sigh, "Oh, guess not. Maybe I should go and get Daisy. You probably want her..."

"No, no, no! We want you, our Puerto Rican princess, not that cheap, used-up Barbie doll." He tosses a large wad of bills and I laugh at his insult, but then frown. "I'm Brazilian, not Puerto Rican. Big difference." I shove him back a little to resume my pole routine. It gets the reaction I want, more money. Whatever it takes during this set. I guarantee even if I made $5000, my brother would still force me to the backroom. It's humiliation; it's blackmail; it's an intimidation tactic.

My last song concludes as I undo my top but reveal nothing. I hold them, take a bow, and wink before turning and walking off. I sigh loudly and wait as security gathers and totals my earnings. Well, his earnings. When I get home, I'm taking whatever I can fit in our bags and run. I don't care if we have to live on the street; it's better than this. I even thought of dropping her off at a firehouse or police station so that someone could give her the life I can't.

But I know I'd die if she weren't with me. If I had never had her, my life would have been much worse; she was my silver lining, my reason to live.

"Well, sis, you made your quota by dancing alone."

I tut, "So, you're still going to force me to suck dick for money. Don't patronize me and act like you give a shit; you only care about your business. I got 30 minutes before your first customer fulfills his dream and solidifies that no one will want me."

I hope you're happy.

"Avi..."

I try to will the tears to stop, but the whole situation's gravity is like a punch in the gut. He wipes my tears and suddenly, I see the remnants of my kind, caring brother, my protector.

Maybe he's remorseful.

Perhaps he does want to fix our relationship and make it...

He disturbingly pats my ass, "Of course you are. You can make close to two grand by shaking your ass; you can probably double that with a few hours back there. Now go, you only have 20 minutes now. And brush your teeth; details matter."

A fucking monster! I sneer at him and stomp away toward the dressing room. I plop down, not even worried about my surroundings.

"Well, well, well...you waltz in here and automatically become a fan favorite. You think you're going to take my crown?!"

I didn't even bother to turn around or look up, "Nobody wants your Queen of the Whores crown but you. You can't be this desperate for my brother's attention, right? Are you here because you want to be his number one, or because he supplies your fucked up habit? You weren't always like this, and I know this because Cullen would never let you fall this far."

"DON'T... you talk about him! You've got his attention now but if I wanted him back, I could."

I chuckle and turn around, "Doubtful because he isn't chasing after you, he's chasing after me. He's a really great guy, too. You see how he defended me and came to my rescue?"

"Shut up! He'll never love you like he loves me."

"But darling, you're not with him and he even said he doesn't want you." I smirk as her face twists up in outrage, but then she laughs, "Well, after tonight, he won't want you either."

I try not to flinch and show how much that hurts. I have to give up on my happily ever after for a 'get the hell out of here' card or even an 'as long as my daughter is safe'. I suck back my feelings and give her an emotionless stare.

"You'll never be his ol' lady."

"You're right. I won't. I don't care anymore; you got it? You two won; I'm stuck in this miserable hell hole making money for my brother. What's worse is working beside you but don't worry, I have no interest in screwing my brother. Your spot on is arm is safe. Now, I need to prepare for my demise if we're done here. I've only got five minutes of my freedom left."

I turn around to finish freshening up my makeup as she babbles behind me.

"I guess it truly does suck to be you. But I'm not satisfied with you only becoming a dick-sucking stripper..." I ignore her until I feel a prick in my arm.

Adrenaline causes me to jump up, knocking my chair back, I rear back and slug her as hard as possible and she slams against the wall. "What'd the fuck did you do, you stupid slut?!" I think my freak-out made it worse. My vision was wavering in and out while I was trying to see how close she was to me to make sure she didn't do anything else.

I hear her laughing, "That'll be the only shot you get at me! Now, who's the druggie whore? Ahahahaha...you're lucky it was only what's left from an earlier hit. Don't you feel it? Coursing through your veins, your heart rate speeding up and your body starting to shake, trying to adjust to the hallucinogen's euphoric feeling. It's magical, isn't it?!"

Laughter, all I hear is her laughing. I had no idea how I was going to recover, would I become like her? "You might break my record of blowing 21 guys in one night, even letting them fuck you. Welcome to my world..."

It's so warm! I can't rip off my clothing; I'd be more susceptible. I am starting to feel tingly all over and it's hard to stand on my feet.

Why are my hands numb?!

I turn to see her walk out of the room, at least the immediate threat was gone but who knows what she has planned. They'll be coming to take me to the champagne room and without all my senses, I could be forced to do anything. I needed help and fast but there are no phones anywhere.

The drug was coursing wildly through my system. I hear a knock and do my best to look normal when the bodyguard steps in. I'm sitting down, but my arms and legs are numb, like I've been sitting in one position for hours.

"Boss wants you to grab them from their seats. First customer is at table four. Fifteen minutes or less for each client, so you better be good or learn to get them off quicker. Let me know when you hit the five-minute mark so I can get my turn." He adjusts himself and I think he's grinning, but I'm not sure. I nod as I try to stay balanced on my heels and walk normally.

Our constant back and forth and not once did I ever think about actually responding with violence toward Daisy, they were verbal threats and catty remarks but now I'm ready to stomp her eight feet under. She's lucky I could only get the one shot in. I should have dragged her ass across the backroom until the floor was covered in her blood and teeth.

Worrying about Raven seeing me like this worsens the effects, so I inhale deeply and close my eyes for a moment. The hallway looks 500 feet long as I place my hand against it for stability. I try to look composed when he glances back to make sure I'm following.

"You, okay?' I place my hand on my forehead and then run it through my hair. "I'm overheated from the floor routine. I just...I just need a glass of ice-cold water." He nods, giving me a sliver of humanity. Then I hear a commotion but I'm so out of it, it could be a hallucination.

My pulse is racing and thumping so loud I can hear and feel it in my ears. My wavering vision is starting to spin as I approach the end of the hallway that opens into the main floor. I'm fighting for my consciousness, but I can't...

I hope this isn't my last memory.

Chapter Thirty-One

Reaper

Despite my blind rage, it feels good to hop on my Betty girl. Lucifer explained the situation to all the Presidents. Two chapters opted to stand guard here, and one would accompany us. The rest, who weren't on their way home, would be outside city limits if Frankie tried to run. We'd call with the code word when we were all clear.

"Reaper." Lucifer rolls up next to me. "Lead the way." I was stunned; the President always leads the crew. I shook my head, but he nodded, "Yes, this mission is different. We're behind you. Be her saving grace, and then we'll discuss next steps."

"'They're with me from now on, even if I have to move out of the clubhouse. I need my girls in my life; I've never been more sure."

He smiles and laughs heartily, "I know, son, I know. We'll figure it out but first, let's get her."

I had a passing thought and I felt I needed to say it. "If anything happens to me, make sure they're taken care of." Then I rev my engine and look down the driveway; no words needed.

I'm sure the roaring engines gave us away, but I didn't care,

we outnumbered them like ten to one. We had the entire establishment surrounded so Frankie couldn't slither away. I see the
doorman relay something over his earpiece. I hop off and march
straight to the entrance.

"You can't come in! Strict orders from the boss, no bikers."

I didn't hesitate to pull my Glock and fire a round into his
knee. Bastard will think twice about associating himself with
Frankie every time he feels pain after his grueling recovery. I
crouch down and cover his mouth to muffle his screaming, to
get my message across. "Tell Frankie he's going to pay for what
he did." He doesn't move, so I cock it again and aim it at his
head, "Tell him! NOW!"

I didn't even wait to hear him relay it as I barged in. People
start running past me to get away from the looming danger.
Dancers are running and screaming, men are pulling their
pants up in a panic. It literally makes my stomach turn to think
what he's got her doing, what any of the girls were doing against
their will.

One of his security guards tried to pull his gun, but I shot
off two rounds, hitting his chest and leg. He falls forward
against the bar. Demon and Fiend move to clear everyone out
to search for Frankie. There's no way that fucker's escaping this
time.

They use a sweeping motion and are about to go down
the hallway when Demon froze. The color drained from his
face.

"Reaper, quick!" Both are now frozen in place and I
see why.

Avi comes into my view, but something is wrong. She is
shaky on her heels in that tiny fabric called a dress; she was
bare to the world. She clung to the wall just to stay upright; she
was breathing hard.

Her eyes met mine when she got to the opening. "Cullen."

She reaches for me, and I dive to catch her before hitting the ground. She was limp in my arms.

"Avi! Avi, wake up! What's wrong with you?" I try to shake her awake. I've never seen her like this and she's not responding.

Demon bends down to offer help, but I don't want anyone touching her. "Call 911!" He dials as he runs outside. Fiend kneels down, but I won't let him touch her either.

"Reap, look." He points to her arm, there's a large red circle with a raised bump. "She's inflamed; I think she's on something. It's a telltale sign, like an allergic reaction. I've seen it when my mom strung out on something new." Her body was giving us clues because there's no way I believe she did this willingly. She would never do drugs, especially with Raven around.

Suddenly she started to groan, barely able to open her eyes. Her hand attempted to touch my face, so I grab her hand. "Are you really here?"

"Yes, darling. Hold on; the ambulance is on its way. Did Frankie do this to you?" She was barely able to shake her head.

"S-she...did." And then she exhaled and went limp again. "Avi...Avi! No!" I hear the sirens approaching, but she's not moving.

"You've got to let me check, Cullen!" Fiend yelled at me as he checked her pulse. "She's not breathing. Lay her down... now! You want her to die? Let me do this!"

I relinquished my hold and lay her down but don't leave her side. Squeezing her hand, hoping for a response. He starts CPR on her, blowing into her. I watch her chest rise and then fall but not continuously as it should. Then he does chest compressions. "Come on, Avi. Come on! Breathe for me! Fight!" He goes back to giving her air. She lurches and he immediately turns her to the side as she retches.

She's breathing on her own. He pats her back, "This is good;

hopefully, it got some of it out of her system, but she's going to have to detox in the hospital."

The paramedics came in with the backboard and trauma bags. Everything is happening so fast.

"What happened?"

"She was injected with something. She threw up, but she did stop breathing earlier. Gave her a round and a half of CPR." He spoke so calmly.

Fiend stands and grabs me by the shoulders while they check her vitals. I know I look out of it.

"Hey, she's going to be fine. The hardest part will be the detox since this is possibly her first time."

I felt anger to think he thought she did things like this. She would never, especially not in front of her daughter.

Oh god.

"What do I tell Raven?"

We're interrupted when they lift her ready for transport. "Are one of you family?"

"I'm her boyfriend. I'm all she has besides her daughter." The EMT nods at me and I follow them out. Fiend joins my brothers, relaying what happened. I could see the worry on all their faces.

They load her in and I look back...

"Don't worry, we'll grab your bike. Go on, son." I see an extra man from the Pennsylvania chapter hop on my girl to get her back home. My brotherhood is strong nationwide. I wouldn't trade them in for anything. I didn't even care if they caught Frankie or not. I know he wouldn't make it out of town.

We get to the emergency room entrance when the monitor emits a long wavering tone. "She's crashing! We've got to get her into ICU stat!" Her hand is ripped from me as they rush her behind the ICU doors.

I'm just standing there.

Numb. Helpless. Lost.

She was dying and I didn't know if they could save her.

He pumped her full of drugs.

No...she said she

She? She...

Then my anger re-emerged.

Daisy.

That strung-up druggie whore! She did this out of jealousy, she didn't want Avi in my life because I didn't want her back in mine.

I finally got the energy to sit and I'm numb to my surroundings. Someone sits next to me, "Sir, can you fill out her paperwork? Fill out what you can." I nod as I glance at the nurse while taking the clipboard.

First name, Avi

Last name, I'm assuming it's Cabrera like Frankie

Address, I jot down mine

I filled out a bit more and listed myself as her emergency contact. I stand up to hand over the clipboard. "Does she have insurance?" I know she doesn't, seeing as she's not even legal. "I'll pay for it, bill it to that address with my name." She nods as she starts typing.

I turn to see a man approach, "Did you come in with the overdose victim?"

"She didn't overdose; she was drugged!" I didn't mean to yell, but she was no addict.

"I apologize. She will need to spend some time detoxing; it should take 2 to 3 days to clear her system. Her heart is trying to overcompensate and that's why she crashed. She'll be on a heart monitor while she recovers. She's almost out of the woods but tonight is critical."

"Can I see her?"

He sighs. I know it was well past visitation hours, but how could I confidently tell Raven her mom was okay?

"She has a daughter, and I can't lie to her. I'm begging you."

"Five minutes, Mr...."

"Anderson. Also, I want it noted that I am her only visitor and her daughter. If any other man comes by, stop him. He's the reason she's in here. Call the cops and me." I looked at him and the nurse to ensure she put it in the file before I followed him.

Would Frankie kill his sister? Abso-fucking-lutely. I'm taking no chances until he takes his last breath.

The walk down the ICU hall is heartbreaking. I wanted to be her Prince and rescue her, but it was too late and she was poisoned. Now my Sleeping Beauty is fighting for her life.

It's not as romantic as the fairytale; she's not lying on a bed surrounded by flowers; she's in a hospital bed surrounded by tubes with needles in her arm.

So many needles...

No birds are chirping, only the beeps and clicks of the machines keeping her stable. I wanted to feel her lips on mine and bring her back to life, but that's not how the real-world works.

"I'll be right outside." The doctor states as he grabs her clipboard.

"Thank you." I pull my chair up and take her hand, squeezing it. "Avi, I'm here. It's Cullen. I will take care of Raven until you're well again. I swear on my life... I'm going to kill your brother for this! I..." I stopped to calm down; she didn't need to feel my anger. She needed positivity.

I kiss her hand, "I just want to be everything you both need. I can do that, Avi. Please come back." I stand up and kiss her forehead. "Your happiness is here with me."

I meant what I said, I had no idea what this was, but I

wanted us to figure it out together. I sigh as I open the door, looking at her beautiful face one more time.

"Thank you, Dr..." I shake his hand.

"Preston. I'll have the nurse call you if any major change happens."

I realized I didn't have my bike. I was about to ask the nurse for the phone but saw Lucifer and Demon half asleep in the waiting area.

I clear my throat and they stand up.

"How is she?"

"She crashed again when we got here but now, she's stable. She's gotta stay to detox. Jeez, I didn't even ask what the substance was." I pull my hair in frustration.

"It was PCP, Mr. Anderson. We just received her lab report." The nurse says.

"Thank you. Let's go; I need to tell my tater tot."

"You think that's a good idea?" Demon asks. I've been contemplating that the entire time. I know I can't lie to her. I shrug my shoulders.

It's super late and I expect her to be asleep. All the visiting clubs have gone home or to the hotel.

We step in and I see Raven wide awake, watching TV in Sam's lap. She threw off the blanket and I stooped down to pick her up.

"Why aren't you asleep?"

"I tried to get her to sleep, but she wanted to wait up for you and...get an update?"

"Did you find my mommy?"

"Yes, I did, but..." I set her down and take her tiny hands in mine. "There was a problem and mommy had to go to the hospital. She has to be there a few days to get better, but I promise I'll take you by tomorrow, okay?"

I tried to prepare for it, but I could never brace for the tears.

She hugged me tighter as she cried and hiccupped. Her body wracked in sobs. "I know, sweetie. I know." I moved to sit in the recliner and rock her. Sam turned down the tv and kissed my forehead. She and Lucifer resigned to their room.

"You need anything?" Demon asks me and I shake my head. A minute later, I checked and she had fallen asleep, her tear-stained face a reminder of all she's endured in her short time.

I'm able to get up and lay her in my bed. I have a stuffed bear my mom gave me when I was six; I placed it under her arm. I turn on my lamp, leave the door open, and lay on the couch.

I don't know how much time had passed, but I woke up when I felt something on top of me. It was a blanket. Sam sat down, "She's still asleep; I checked. I figured you'd sleep out here."

"Why aren't you asleep?"

"Are you kidding? When you said her mother was in the hospital, my heart broke. What happened?"

"Daisy drugged her. She flatlined twice, but now she's stable. The next 24 hours are crucial to her recovery. She has to detox and it shocked her heart so much she'll have to wear a monitor. What is going on in my life, Sam? This isn't the life of a hardcore biker."

She scoffed, "Who said you had to be a stereotypical biker? What does that even mean anyway? Plenty of the guys here are family men; those were their wives, not just their ol' lady; they have kids and grandkids. Being a biker is a part of their life, not their WHOLE life. Now, you vowed to protect her and that child..."

"And I mean it. But there are so many emotions!" I yell but then catch myself, "I'm angry, pissed that Frankie and Daisy are breathing. I want vindication! I don't want them to live in fear because that bastard and that bitch are still alive! I want to end this bloodily and violently. But I also don't want to end up in jail. I want to be there for them every day from today on."

"I knew I didn't like that dirty, manipulative bitch for a reason. What if she would've killed her?! If I ever see her again...." She rubs her temples, trying to stay quiet, so Raven can sleep. She drops her hands, "Your heart was too good for her. Now, take that healed heart and focus on your new family."

That jolted me a bit. Was that it? Did I now have a makeshift family? It was a lot to take in but not off-putting in the least bit.

"I'm going to try and get some sleep. I'll be up early to get a big breakfast going. Try to rest, okay?"

"Thank you for watching her."

"Are you kidding? It's nice to have a precocious little girl around. Maybe I will have someone call me grandma after all." Her face lights up at the thought.

The ordeal caught up with me and I dozed off hard and fast.

Some hours later, I hear Sam quietly trying to maneuver around in the kitchen. As I was about to get up and check on Raven, I realized she was lying on me. Not sure when that happened but I pulled the blanket to cover her. I noticed the bear in her hand. I refrain from moving and settle on watching her sleep, hoping her mother's condition improved overnight. I'm not a praying man, but I did my best last night asking for mercy. Maybe I would call the hospital first before taking her down there.

I'm lost in my thoughts till I feel her move. "*Mamae...*" She shifts and I use that movement to lay her on the couch. I yawn and stretch as I make my way into the kitchen, "What time is it?"

"It's 7:45 a.m. I came out and she was on your chest; it was the most heartwarming thing. I may have taken a picture or two." She squeals happily as I roll my eyes before going to brush my teeth. I take a quick shower and change. When I return, the television is on some kid show and I see her rocking happily, eating a banana.

"Hey, tater tot, you sleep okay?"

"Uh-huh. I'm sad about *mamae*. Is she going to die?" She said it so innocently I wondered if she had witnessed death before. "No, she's fighting hard to get back to you. She needs some help from the doctors, okay?"

"Do I have to go back to Uncle Frankie's? I hate him! He hit mama, then he hit me. He took away my friend Diesel. He went to heaven. *Mamae* was very sad. I was, too."

It sounds like, did he kill someone in front of her?

I was about to ask, but there was a knock. I see Sam come from the kitchen when I open the door. I'm face to face with two officers.

"Mr. Cullen Anderson?"

"Yes."

"We got a tip that you are in possession of a large amount of cocaine. We have a warrant to search your room and your belongings."

My head was swimming, "I what?!"

"Yes, specifically..." He thumbs through his notepad, "in your bike. Can you show me to it, please?" I groaned and Sam looked concerned. "It's fine; watch Raven." She mouthed okay. I know she's going to get Lucifer.

We headed to the garage where she was parked. The officer wore gloves before opening the saddlebags, checking around the back tire, and flashing a light down the tailpipe. Then he wiggled my seat and stuck his hand in, producing a bag of white powder. "Do you know anything about this, Mr. Anderson?"

"If I did, do you think I would have led you to it?! No! Somebody planted that on my bike. It had to be while I was in the hospital and my family brought my bike home. I'll kill that son-of-a-bitch!"

He didn't look convinced, but I know who's trying to set me up. To get me locked away so he can continue to torture Avi and Raven or worse, get rid of them. I can tell you that even if I went to prison, my brothers would never let him within ten feet of my girls!

"Mr. Anderson, we're going to have to put you under arrest for possession of an illegal substance."

"This is bullshit!" I scream after they cuff me and lead me to the squad car. Lucifer approached, but the other cop stopped him as they put me in the car. I can see him try to negotiate but judging by the head shaking, it wasn't going well.

We lock eyes, "I'll be right there, son."

"Take care of Raven." I didn't care about this trumped-up charge. It wouldn't stick after I told my side.

Down at the station, they put me in an interrogation room. They're observing me from the other side, we know how this works, but I wouldn't show guilt. There is none. I'd wait for them to give up and come in.

Fifteen minutes later, the Chief of police comes in,

"Cullen."

"Chief Grady. This is horse shit!"

"Tell me what happened."

"Frankie Cabrera happened and don't lie and say he isn't the one who 'tipped you off'. I know for a fucking fact he's setting me up!"

I found out they arrested Frankie on numerous charges after the night club fiasco and had him arraigned here.

"What would be his motive?"

I leaned forward and scoffed, "Plenty, that bastard has had

it in for me for protecting his sister, showing her affection because all he wants to do is control and torture her and her daughter. He's verbally and physically abusive toward them. Ask his niece! She came to me with a clear handprint on her face. You'd be trying to identify pieces of his body if it weren't for the incident at his club where his girlfriend whore drugged his sister."

He leans back, "That's a big accusation. But then, what about the cocaine?"

"Frankie is a drug lord! Check his strip club, his drop houses, hell, check his shipments that come in from Brazil. I guarantee you'll find evidence that he's moving huge payloads."

They can't be that blind to his operation.

"We've been trying to locate the drop houses for months, but we can't pinpoint them."

"Avi knows. He forced her to work for him. She could tell you his whole operation."

"A mole could blow this whole thing wide open. Where is she?"

"She's in the hospital battling for her life. The doctor says she needs to detox, but I swear to you she knows."

He rubs his face, "Let's hope she pulls through. She could be a critical asset to this case. Everything is being routed up to the DOJ and USCIS because there is no legal paperwork for a Frankie Cabrera anywhere, no ID, license, or birth certificate. Also, know that the Brazil police department has an APB on him. He could be extradited."

"Good fucking riddance."

He holds up the bag, "But let's talk about a deal because we have no evidence to prove that this doesn't belong to you. This could get you 10 to 15 years in federal prison. I'll need a full statement from you and his sister. And I mean everything, Cullen. I know you've done some business for him that's not exactly on the up and up. Let's work together to send him away."

I neglected to think about our part in all his dealings. We could be facing charges. This piece of shit could still drag us down with him. "I'll take a piss test or a lie detector test. Whatever it takes to keep us out of trouble. I've got a little girl to take care of now. I'm all she has while her mom is in the hospital."

It's the sympathy card, but Chief Grady knows us and what we stand for. Our noses aren't clean, but we're not hardened criminals.

"I'll tell you what, you give me your story, full details and I'll release you to Rocco and Sam's custody. Do not leave city limits, Cullen. You may have to appear in court."

"I'm not leaving my girls." Chief Grady sets down the recorder and I tell them everything from when I first met Frankie's sniveling face. I knew he'd throw us under the bus. He's only looking out for himself. Even Daisy isn't safe from Frankie stabbing her in the back, which I could care less about. I made sure to ask them to search her residence and locker at the club for proof she drugged Avi maliciously.

It took two almost three hours before they released me to Lucifer, who was in the waiting area.

"This is the second time I've had to ask if you're okay." I guess he saw the worried look on my face. I had to admit to squealing like a pig, I felt like I was no better than Frankie. But I had a family to take care of now but I still felt guilty.

"I'm sorry, Boss, I had to tell them everything. I can't let him get away with what he did. I told you he'd tried to take us down with him!"

"You did. And that's okay; I wouldn't expect you to lie. Besides, Chief Grady and I have a long relationship and he knows about all our runs. This investigation has been going on for quite a long time. Slow and steady wins the race." He pats my back and I'm shocked!

Lucifer's been here his whole life, I should have known he put down roots, but I didn't expect him to have an in with the police chief.

On the way home, I called the hospital for an update and was told she's showing the physical effects of withdrawal, but she's still fluttering in and out of consciousness. I would have to break Raven's heart and tell her she couldn't see her mother. I didn't want her to see her shaking, cold, and sweaty.

When we return, I see the brothers put together a makeshift swing out of rope and an old tire. She's squealing and asking to go higher. Demon pushes and puts a little spin on it, causing her to giggle more. So innocent.

They slow the swing down so she can get off and the moment she sees me. Her and her pigtails run right into my arms.

"I'm dizzy! I like the swing they made for me." She's smiling so widely, how do I break it to her? I need to be honest. "Looks like fun. Listen, princess, I know I said we were going to see mommy today, but the doctor said she wasn't ready for visitors."

"Oh...okay." She was super disappointed, but it was for the sanity of her innocence.

"But I'll call tomorrow and maybe they'll let you come? They did say she was doing better, but she's still sleeping. She needs her rest to get better."

"Okay! I said a prayer for *mamae* so she could come home. Will...will we live with you? Here?"

"For now, tater tot. Your mom and I will have to talk."

"Are you going to send us away?!" Panic washed over her face. I realize I didn't say that correctly.

"No, I meant maybe we could find a place together if my

room can't hold all 3 of us. I would never send you away, sweetie."

"Yay!" She wraps her tiny arms around my neck.

"I'm going to take her some flowers and tell her you're okay. What kind should I buy her?"

I know roses are the default, but maybe I could personalize them.

"She likes all kinds of flowers. She'll like whatever you get her."

"Okay, I'll make you proud." I wink and she makes a cute attempt to wink back but merely closes both eyes tightly.

Sam comes out of the house onto the porch, "Raven, darling, come help the girls and me with lunch so we can feed the hungry bikers."

"Yay, I help!" She trots off to hold Sam's hand. The bunnies follow behind them. It's funny how the whole dynamic can change with a child around. The girls pulled their skirts down and untied their shirts. They're in awe of such a sweet little girl.

They were all little girls once.

"Hey, I'm headed to the hospital." The guys nod and I'm on my bike, hoping to see her eyes when I open the door.

I picked up a dozen pink tulips in a green-tinted vase. They smell amazing and I hope she'll enjoy the fragrance. I said hello to the receptionist nurse, letting her know where I was going. She warns me that detox isn't pretty and to be supportive.

I knock but hear no response. When I opened the door, her eyes did meet mine, but her body shaking was very obvious in response to the detox.

"I-I-I don't want you to to s-see me like this this." She looked away.

"Avi..."

"No! Get out...please!" She squeaked out, letting the tears fall as she continued to look away.

I set down the tulips on her food tray and grabbed her hand. "Hey, look at me..." I try to hold her hands still. She looks at our joined hands. "How could you...wa-want someone li-li-like me? A stripper with a kid."

"You're a strong woman willing to sacrifice for your daughter and that's the most beautiful thing. I'm not judging what you've done because I know why you did it."

"She's n-not here is..."

"No, I told her mommy needed her rest. She was very upset, but I thought it was best." She nods in agreement, shudders, and pulls the cover up her neck. "So cold." I didn't hesitate to pull her toward me and she sighed, her shaking starting to diminish. I rub her scalp and she's asleep in no time.

All is peaceful until the nurse comes in with lunch. "Make sure she tries to eat. At least the bread to settle her stomach and I got her ginger ale." The nurse whispered.

"Okay." I nudged my shoulder, "Avi, baby, wake up." Her eyes open and she smiles, then she rips off her blanket. "It's hot! Argh, I hate this!"

"I know, but you're getting better. Yesterday you... I almost lost you. So, I'm not going to leave you to fight this alone and when you're cleared, you'll come home."

"H-home?" She looked up at me and I felt the urge, so I leaned down and kissed her. It was slow and full of passion, the perfect kiss despite the circumstances.

"Yes, home. I hope you're okay living with someone with a record." She raised her brow, confused by my statement. "Your brother planted drugs in my bike and I was arrested today."

"He's not my brother or my family! I only have Raven. You'd understand if I told you what he did to us. I'm starting my life over a-again without his so-called help. I hope he dies a painful, mis-miserable, slow-burning d-death!"

I reached for her food tray trying to distract her from her

anger which seemed to exasperate her symptoms. "I need you to eat something."

She shook her head, "I didn't keep breakfast down and I don't want them cleaning up after me. I can't even walk to the bathroom and this stupid heart monitor is so annoying!" She taps the white device taped to her chest. I don't think it was actually annoying her, but she was frustrated being in this cold room away from her daughter.

"I promise I will help you. I'll carry you to the bathroom and hold your hair, but you've got to try to eat something. It'll help get the drugs out of your system." I'm pretty sure that's not true, but whatever it takes. She takes the roll, takes a tiny bite, swallows it, and puts it back.

"Really?"

"Give it a few minutes. This whole situation has been hell because Frankie didn't want me with you. He wanted me to offer up my body to his patrons for a price. He gave me a $1,000 quota that night and was going to make me work the champagne room after my stage performance. My sweet, protecting brother died long before I came here and met this monster."

Everything she reveals only exasperates my rage, "I'm going to kill him, Avi, I swear!" She flinched when I raised my voice. She pats my chest; Beauty was calming down her Beast. "No. I don't want you to go down with him; then what would I do? What would I tell Raven?"

Which reminded me, "The Chief of police wants to talk to you about his operation. They've been trailing him and gathering info to take him down. In the meantime, he's throwing us under the bus like I knew the coward would, but Lucifer has a lot of pull in this town. Hopefully, we won't face any jail time but if I do, you'll stay with Sam. Sam loves Raven; she's the perfect grandma. They cook together and watch movies. She's safe."

I watched her face fall, feeling like she was being replaced. "Don't think that way; she's asked about you every chance she's gotten. I know her face will light up once I tell her she can come to see you tomorrow. If you still have symptoms, we can make up a story."

"No, I've never sugar-coated our life in Maua and I won't do it now. She's a tough little cookie who knows that hard times are temporary and always finds the good in situations. I can't wait to hold her. I miss her so much. Wait, how did she end up with you?"

"Oh, about that... don't freak out, while I was trying to figure a way to get you out of there, she burst through the club-house door. She ran there. She looked so scared and she ran into my arms. She said she snuck out of the window of her room after the butler locked her up. I knew then I wouldn't let her go back, either of you. I've taken care of her; she even slept on my chest, a closeness I never felt before. Here..." I hand her the roll and she nibbles on it since she didn't get sick. She points to the ginger ale and I pour a small amount.

The doctor walks in with a chart, "Ms. Cabrera, it's good to see you eating. How do you feel? Hello, again, Mr. Anderson."

"I still get the shakes and I get cold, then hot. How long will it last? And how long do I have to wear this monitor?"

"With PCP, it's a shorter recovery period than the harder barbiturates. The average time is two to three days; judging your symptoms right now, you should be over the hump. You may still experience things like headaches and muscle soreness. The next week or two should be taken very easy. I know you have a daughter but no picking her up, you hear me? As for the monitor we just want to make sure the heart is operating as it should after being thrown into arrest."

She was about ready to fuss about Raven, but I stopped her, "Doctors orders, baby. She'll understand. Doc, can I bring her with me tomorrow?"

"Sure, I think tomorrow could be your last day being admitted. I'll get your prescriptions ready for you to take home and Mr. Anderson, you understand everything will be billed to you?"

I nod and the doctor turns and leaves. "I can't let you pay for this! It's going to cost a fortune! I'll never be able to pay you back."

"It's fine. Not like they're taking it all at once. Don't worry about money, I'm okay. We'll be okay."

Her beautiful smile finally appeared. "I like when you say we. I never stopped thinking about that first kiss. It was magical. I want that and more." She pulled me down unexpectedly, she was pretty strong, but for a kiss like this, she could do whatever she wanted. She's smiling hard when we separate. "Thank you for saving me, for taking care of my daughter."

"My tater tot."

"Yeah, you'll never get rid of her now."

"And I'm never letting her go, or you. Get some rest and I'll bring her by tomorrow. Please try to eat more, okay?"

"Okay. Thank you for the flowers; they're beautiful."

"Not as beautiful as you. Night."

I'm glad I can give my little tater tot some good news.

Chapter Thirty-Two
Avi

I asked the nurse for the Sheriff's number to have him get my statement immediately. At first, I worried I would be extradited, but I equally worried about what the drugs did to my memory. He informed me he'd put in paperwork and a written statement to obtain amnesty for us.

With that reassurance, I mapped out Frankie's entire operation for the next hour and a half. He was so adamant about giving me so many jobs, I was able to describe where his drop houses were and the underground warehouse.

I revealed what was really going on at his strip club, soliciting and prostitution. "If I hadn't passed out, he would have had me taking clients in the back room. All the girls are forced to please clients. There are security cameras, but I'm not sure they're functional; you should seize them. Maybe there's evidence of my drugging. I want that bitch to rot in jail!"

"I know, Cullen said to search her residence and locker to use the findings against her. We got the warrant for her and are working on getting it for Frankie since he has many properties, including his cargo ships. The search could take up to a month to look at it all."

"Whatever it takes to take him down. He's another predator, a monster. What will happen to Cullen and the guys for doing some jobs for Frankie?"

"I'm not at liberty to say, but I have some contacts higher up and I can vouch for them. Lucifer and I went to school together. I know he's a good guy who took the boys in. Nobody's perfect. I know you're still recovering from the attack, so I want you to write down anything you might remember from now until the arraignment. You are the key to full prosecution."

"I know. Thank you, Chief." He tips his hat and I feel the weight off my shoulders but there's a looming danger. I constantly look over my shoulder because I don't feel safe, even here. I feel like I'll wake up looking down the barrel of a gun before Frankie pulls the trigger without hesitation. I requested security for that reason and he said he'll send two officers here within the hour. It'll be the most nerve-wracking hour of my life. I know he's locked up but he could bond out with the amount of money he has. As long as he's breathing, I'll never feel safe.

Emotionally and mentally drained, I nodded off, dreaming of my sweet little girl. Watching as she slept on his chest. It was the daddy/daughter moment I longed for her to have.

She was comfortable in her surroundings and not afraid that someone would enter the bedroom or having to lock the doors behind me. She was safe...she was sound...

click

The noise startles me out of my dream and it's exactly like my nightmare as I'm looking down the barrel of a gun. My brother smirked as I took in his clothing, t-shirt and sweatpants. I thought he was behind bars. Did he escape?

"Don't make a fucking sound." The scream threatening to roar forward came out as a squeak behind my hands. I had to find a way to alert anyone outside.

My shaking re-emerged in my fear-laden state and I crossed my arms and put my hands in my underarms.

"Fr-Frankie, what are you doing here?"

"You'd be nothing without me, Avi! I'm going to make my problem go away and they'll have no key witness to put me away!"

I decided to distract him while I slowly lowered my arms.

"Where i-is Rav-raven? Is she okay? Did you bring her? I want to see her! Please!"

I saw him hesitate. I wanted to see if he would flat-out lie. I exaggerate my shaking so that he won't notice my hand slide over to the side of my leg.

"She's fine where she is, for now. Because of your little boyfriend and his gang, they raided my club. If I go down, they're going down with me. Then you'll have no one, so why shouldn't I put a bullet in your head and then go home, corner her in your room, and laugh before I shoot her execution style? I'll get away with it too because I'll be on a ship so fast, they'll never find me." He laughed and it was sinister, but it kept him occupied while I reached under and pressed the nurses' call button. I had to improvise my next move because I didn't want anyone to get hurt. I had to take the risk and create a diversion.

I started laughing; it was low and deep. Frankie stopped to observe me. "What the fuck are you laughing about?! I'm going to kill you! You should be begging for your pathetic life and that of your little brat."

My shaking stopped and my adrenaline pumping, "You're a god damned liar, Frankie! Raven isn't with you; she hasn't been in that house for almost two days! You're such a fucking coward! You'd kill your sister and your niece because you're going down for the life you chose?! Fuck you, Frankie! I wish I had never come here looking for you! But I do relish knowing two things you don't: Raven is safe in her new home with Cullen and..." I squeeze the buzzer again and two cops come in with their guns raised, "Drop your weapon!"

He growled before dropping the gun. I smirk, "and two, you'll never hurt us again. I hope you die a painful death. You're a disgrace to mom and dad. You're a disgrace to the Cabrera bloodline!"

He lunged at me, but they held him tighter before cuffing him and escorting him out. After the adrenaline wore off, the shock set in and I cried hysterically as the nurse tried to calm me down.

"Get her file and call, Mr. Anderson, now!"

Chapter Thirty-Three
Reaper

"Tell me what other types of animals live in the sea?"

She ponders for only a split second. "Seahorses, starfish, and umm... lobsters! Did you know that parts of the ocean are not discovered!"

I tap her nose, "Undiscovered, sweetie. Instead of not discovered."

"Undiscovered. Oh, ok. Can I watch Discovery channel?"

I nodded, then she glanced over at Lucifer. "Can I sit with you?" I think she's grown really fond of him. He has pop-pop written all over, or pawpaw, maybe grandpa. Guess it's his decision what he'd like to be called especially since she'll probably become his permanent shadow.

He put out his cigar and held his arms out. "Of course, kiddo. Come on, let's learn about dolphins."

"Yay, dolphins!" She ran over with a blanket and snuggled up against him in his leather recliner. They comfortably watched the program. I don't think I've ever seen him so gentle.

It's kind of sad he and Sam never had kids, but they definitely make amazing grandparents and surrogate parents for this band of misfits.

I'm startled by my phone buzzing, "Hello?"

"Mr. Anderson, it's Charlene from the hospital; there's been an incident. We need you here now!"

I was already marching towards the door before I hung up.

"Hey, what's going on?!" Fiend shouted; I think. I didn't care to look back.

"Hospital, something happened." Then I stopped cold when I realized Raven heard me. I'm furious at myself for being so careless with my words. I turned around to see she had jumped off Lucifer's lap with tears in her eyes, "*Mamae?*" She squeaked.

"Come here. I promise, she's okay."

She started to pound her fists against me. "NO! I want to see *mamae*! I want to see my mommy!" Begging with me to take her, but I would be bringing her into an unknown situation. What if something DID happen? Then I remember Avi said she never sugar-coated incidents that happened back home and I'm going to respect that.

"Raven, hey, stop. I'll take you, okay? But you got to be a big, brave girl. Can you do that?" She wipes her face and sniffles a bit before nodding. I take her hand and we head outside.

"Wait up!" Fiend runs behind us, "I'm going with you. Don't argue with me; let's go." He takes Raven's hand, lifts her into the truck, and buckles her in.

I wanted to peel out of there recklessly, but I had precious cargo with me. There were so many scenarios going on in my head. I feared most that she was dead; she was gone. I don't know what I would do. I try to repress the negativity.

We get there in less than ten minutes, hop out, and rush inside with Raven on my hip. The second we rounded the corner; I'm blinded in rage. I set her down and she scurried behind me.

Now I know why they called me because Frankie is here in handcuffs. I didn't think, I went completely nuclear.

"You motherfucker! I'm going to kill you! You worthless piece of shit!" I managed to snap his head back a couple times before the stopped protecting him to restrain me.

"Stop it! Stooooop!" Raven screaming at the top of her lungs shook me. Hadn't she witnessed and lived through enough?

I shake them off of me, step back, and breathe heavily to calm down. Then I look Frankie dead on, with his newly busted nose and lip, "I'm going to make sure you never see them again. Get him out of my face before I go to jail, not because of your little trumped-up drug charges either. Nice try, motherfucker." I chuckle when he jerked to try and get loose.

I grab Raven and carry her tightly, facing her away from him. I'm going to make sure she doesn't fear the boogeyman anymore.

I opened the door to see Avi crying on the nurse's shoulder.

"*Mamae!*" Raven tried to jump out of my arms immediately. Avi looked and held her arms open, begging for that much-needed missed connection between a mother and child. I set Raven on the bed and Avi hugged her so tightly. "My sweet baby, what are you doing here?"

I relented, "She wouldn't let me come alone, she demanded. Tell me what happened." It's hard to dissipate my anger while mentally wanting the satisfaction of causing Frankie's last ragged breath.

Avi leaned back, cradling Raven like a baby while she played in her mother's hair. "I woke up and he had a gun aimed at my head, ready to shoot," I knew she refrained from using the word kill, but he wanted to kill her. "I verbally lashed out, at the same time, I was able to push the call button. I didn't want a nurse to come in and get hurt. I stalled enough for the cops who were supposed to guard me to come and grab him. They have everything on CCTV. That's how they knew he was in my room with a weapon."

I hear a knock and Fiend peeks his head in. "Can I come in?"

"Yeah, Avi, this is Jett, but we call him Fiend."

"Nice to meet you. I talked to the doctor on call and the cops, and she can go home with us tonight. They are gathering her meds and issuing a cane for her to use because of her stability issues. She might not have to wear the monitor; we'll see what the doctor says before we leave." She scoffs, but I look at her. "That's great. Call Sam and let her know to prepare my room for me, please."

"Will do."

I look over and Raven is peacefully sleeping, clutching her mom's hand. Avi squeezes my hand gaining my attention, "Cullen, are you sure about this? There's a lot of responsibility here. I don't want you to feel pressured. You can put us in a hotel until I figure something out. You don't have to..." I listen to her make excuses as to why I shouldn't take care of them. I leaned over and kissed her, gazing into her beautiful eyes; she was blushing.

"No way, darlin', you're mine. We'll talk about that later. First, let's get you home." I touch her forehead to mine and we share a peaceful moment.

We're out of the hospital a half hour later with a cane and meds in Fiend's hand while I push her out in a wheelchair with Raven asleep on her lap. The doctor didn't require her to wear the monitor but insisted she take it easy.

With some maneuvering, we're all inside the truck and headed home. Fiend takes Raven and I carry Avi. She laughs, "This is definitely not the way I wanted to be carried over the threshold." It gives me a flash forward of the possible future.

I set her down in the living room and Fiend hands over Raven. She thanks him as she adjusts comfortably on the couch. Sam comes out of my room and smiles, "You must be her mother, I'm Sam and I can't tell you how much I love having this sweet girl around. I know it's a lot to take in, but you are more than welcome here. Cullen, we shifted the bed against the wall and inflated the air mattress and I had plenty of sheets and blankets. You guys have been through enough today. Go get some rest."

I picked her up and set her on my bed, "You and Raven take the bed and I'll take the mattress."

She shook her head, "No, put her on the mattress. I want... I want to fall asleep and wake up in your arms."

I go back and get Raven and lay her on the mattress, find my teddy bear, and, like before, put him under her arm. She tossed a bit before returning to her peaceful slumber, hugging him a bit tighter.

I set out all of Avi's meds and read them. I needed to know her schedule to make sure she didn't miss a dose.

"Umm, Cullen. I need something to sleep in. All my stuff is at Frankie's." I smile inside thinking that she'll be wearing one of my shirts to sleep in. I'd want to wear it the next day to have her scent on me, to mark me as hers.

I toss her my favorite vintage Metallica shirt. She starts to peel out of the gown and I turn away. I sigh hard as I strip down to my boxers and walk into the bathroom to put my clothes in the hamper.

It wasn't until I saw her sitting innocently in my bed that I realized the difference in this particular situation. In any other case, I'd relish in a beautiful woman in my bed but know she'd be gone before morning. This...was different because I looked over and saw a beautiful little girl sleeping...and there was her mother. Our connection was more emotional than physical. Don't get me wrong, the physical anticipation was there; my libido raging at the sight of her in just my shirt. She lay on the side against the wall and pulled the blanket back. I felt the heated sexual tension as she stared back at me, her eyes shifting slightly lower. I am only wearing boxers and she's half-naked in my bed.

Without words, I slip into bed, laying like I usually do, on my back, hands behind my head. I thought she'd straighten up and lay beside me, but instead, she leaned over and placed her hand on my chest, right on my chapter tattoo. Her touch sent electricity through my body and there was a physical hitch in my breathing. She lay half her body over me, the warmth sooth-ing, sensual, and torturous at the same time. Turning my face toward her, she kissed me and then looked at me while brushing her fingers across my lips. Oh, I wanted to explore every delectable inch of her body and listen to her moan my name, but tonight wasn't the time. Not because of Raven but the trauma they've both endured.

"I know what you're thinking..." She whispered.

"What am I thinking?"

"You're fantasizing about our first time together."

We both look down and I can't deny it either way. I shift and tuck my problem away.

"I...was, but now isn't the time. You're still recovering; you've been through a traumatic few months and I can only imagine what happened back home. We have time for all of that to happen. Besides, I've been thinking about how fast tables have turned and how they've changed my life. After someone, who shall remain nameless," I kiss her forehead, I know she wouldn't want to hear Daisy's name, and I didn't want to give her that power. "After she broke my heart and caused me to wreck my Betty girl, I wasn't ready to open up, I wasn't expecting this. That sweet little girl made me see life through her eyes and to see love in its purest form. She's perfect; I fell in love with her."

"And me? I'm not expecting you to say you love me because I know it would be way too soon."

"Let's just say I was intrigued by you from the moment you cursed me out."

"I shouldn't have taken it out on you. I'm sorry." She interrupted me.

"Contrary to popular belief, it riled me up. I had such a hard-on I may have mistakenly called your name when I was with someone else. I was hooked; that dirty mouth and take no prisoner attitude was what I needed. I want to explore this so much more. Hopefully, I won't spend a good chunk in jail."

"That's not fair!" She tried to whisper yell.

"It's law, sweetheart. Don't worry, you'd still be taken care of. You, Sam, and the girls."

She squeezed me not wanting to talk about it anymore and we lay in silence.

"Did you sleep with any of the girls here?"

Yikes.

I shifted awkwardly; it was going to come to light eventually.

"Only my closest friend, Lila. A couple of times, but she has a boyfriend now. She made it crystal clear it was only for me to vent my frustration. No feelings were involved. You'll meet her soon enough. She's the one that told me I was into you. Well, her, Fiend, Demon, etc., etc. I have a feeling you two will be good friends."

"As long as she's no longer competition. I'm sure I'll get all the dirty details and find out what you like."

She giggles as I roll over halfway, cradling her in my arms. Her arms wrap around me as she snuggles in.

"Mmm, kiss me to sleep, please."

And I did. I alternated between her forehead and lips, basking in her sighs that were borderline moans of pleasure. I continued until she didn't purse her lips then I shifted to her forehead until I, too, fell into a deep sleep.

Chapter Thirty-Four
Avi

I couldn't stop myself from smiling as he slept soundly when I opened my eyes. He was on his back and snoring. One of his hearty snores woke Raven and she couldn't help but giggle and laugh.

"Shhh." I point toward the door and she gets out of bed. I wiggle my legs and am happy to be able to feel them. I use my cane to help me stand up. I'm still weak but not bedridden and that was a start. I look through his drawers to find some shorts. They were huge, but I folded them and made them work. I whisper for her to open the door for me and I follow her towards the living room. She seems comfortable navigating this place. Then she makes a left turn into the kitchen, and I follow.

"Morning, Miss Sam. Did you meet my *mamae*?"

Sam stops and kisses her head, "Morning, tater tot! Yes, I did, last night while you were sleeping. Morning Avi, did you sleep okay?"

I maneuvered onto the stool and leaned against the counter, "Yes, I'm so glad to be out of that hospital. Now I need to figure out how to get us some clothes. We don't have anything." I felt a moment of hopelessness.

"Oh, no problem. I got up super early and got you some basic supplies. I got her some outfits and a few comfortable shirts and tops for you. You look the same size as one of my girls, so I hope I guessed right! Your recovery should be filled with good memories, not rehashing the past and I didn't want you to go back to that horrible place. Raven, why don't you wash up then come back and help me." With a quick okay, Raven disappeared.

I look at Sam, she has a sweet soul, a motherly figure and with a house full of men, she's probably the sanity.

"Sam, I really can't thank you enough for what you've already done." I felt a wayward tear and wiped it away. She comes around and hugs me. I feel her pat my back which comforts me.

"When my sweet boy told me about you, I knew there was something there, a spark. He smiled for the first time after the break-up and accident. Even though your encounter wasn't the most positive, he still smiled. Out of all my boys, he has the biggest heart; take extra special care of it." She started to sniffle and wipe her eyes.

"I will."

Several minutes later, Raven's little footsteps come roaring forward. She's in black leggings and a tunic-style dress with flowers. "Look, it's so pretty!"

"Yes, you are. Did you wash your face and brush your teeth?"

"Si, *mamae*! Look, cheese!" Showing me her pearly whites. "Good, you help Miss Sam and I'm going to get dressed."

I slowly made my way to the hallway bathroom, seeing my stuff in the bag; she had everything. I grabbed it and opened the door to his room to see he wasn't in bed.

Wrecked

I hear water running. I walk into the bathroom and see him brushing his teeth. I take my bag and pull out a toothbrush and hold it out towards him; he grabs the toothpaste squeezing some on my brush. "Thank you." He nods as he goes to pour a pink bubble bath soap into the tub of running water. I spit out the excess and chuckle. "I didn't take you for a bath person."

He cages me against the sink. I don't know if he sprayed cologne or if it's his natural scent, but he smells wonderful. He leans down giving me a quick peck. "The bath is for you. I want you to finally relax. I'll be back in 15 or 20 minutes; call me if you need me."

I wanted him to ravish me and then join me so I could lay against him. I look up and I'm almost certain he could read my mind.

He shook his head, "Don't tempt me, darlin'." He gave me one last kiss before turning off the faucet and closing the door.

The water was perfectly heated. It allowed me to relax my muscles and for my mind to drift. I began to remember things I couldn't recall because of the drug-filled haze. I recognized that the way Cullen felt about my brother is how I felt about Daisy. I hadn't forgotten about what that bitch did to me! She wanted me to be a coked-up tragedy like her, so he wouldn't want me. She's the one that screwed up their relationship, not me. I didn't come and take him. No, she was already with my brother.

I sigh and splash water across my face trying to think of anything that is not negative. I let my hands slide down my stomach. The soft touch was pleasurable, especially after last night's intense stare-down and those boxers that covered nothing. His erection poked me throughout the night while he cuddled me, I was so tempted to palm him, but I didn't, leaving me a throbbing mess.

I'm so wound up that a quick session would relieve some of

my sexual frustration. I could focus on growing together instead of needing him to claim me on the bathroom counter.

My warm, soft fingers ignite the fire in the pit of my stomach, the feeling almost euphoric. It had been so long. My fingers tweaking my nipples, they're more sensitive than I remember and I cry out, "Oh God..." My other hand travels down until I'm feeling fireworks from finding my spot. I speed up, slow down, back and forth. It's intense as I'm gasping to keep from moaning. At my climax, I bite my hand and shudder almost violently, the water nearly splashing to the floor. The relief that washed over me was incredible; my mind felt clear. I washed up quickly and pulled the drain.

I couldn't wait to be in a family-style breakfast setting for the first time. A family setting...with my daughter.

Chapter Thirty-Five
Reaper

I didn't intend to watch her. I had come back to put away my cut. Lucifer called a quick church session in the barn to discuss our current circumstances and the possibility of criminal charges.

The highlight for them, of course, was ragging on me for becoming a 'family man' from where I was only weeks ago. I take it in good humor because this is what I didn't know I needed. I felt myself smiling hard, and they heckled me further. Lucifer dismissed us and I wanted to put my cut away. Maybe wash my hands to help with breakfast, but I think the ladies had it covered, so I checked to see if Avi needed help, especially with her mobility being restricted a bit.

I stood silent trying to gauge her muffled sighs, but not interrupt or go barging in if she wasn't in need of help. I'd look like a perv. But then she squeaked and it raised my suspicion so I peered through the tiny crack in the door and saw her massage her breast. She's probably just washing up, nothing sexual about it at...

Then she pinched her nipple, her other hand suspiciously

out of view until her knees slammed together, her body shook, and she quickly bit her hand to muffle the orgasm that rocked her...

FUCK! I immediately stiffen and it's uncomfortable pressed against my jeans. I need to get this down because there's no way I can rub one out before she's done. I pace the floor and think about anything that doesn't have to do with what I saw.

Puppies, kittens, football, pirates...

Then I hear Raven, Sam, and the girls singing quirky children's songs. That helped. I adjust myself, then knock on the door, "Hey, you need any help?"

I could tell by the way the water splashed around that I startled her. "Huh?! No, I'm almost done. I'll be out in five minutes." I sit in the chair and wait for her, trying my best not to flash back to only moments ago. I almost doze off until the door squeaks and she came out carrying her cane instead of using it.

"Avi..." I scold her with her name.

"I'm fine. The bath was much needed for my recovery."

I bet it was. Relaxing all your tight and tense muscles, relieving most of that stress with your two little fingers.

I'd give anything to taste her fingertips and sample her sweet essence.

"Cullen, you, okay?" I shake my head, realizing I was fantasizing right in front of her. I pull her against me, "Fine, ready to eat? I'll introduce you to everyone."

We walk hand in hand into the dining room. She leans against me, but her grip tightens when all eyes are focused on us.

"Everyone, this is Avi. You know Sam, she's Rocco's wife. That's Rocco known as Lucifer, our club President. You know

Jett aka Fiend, then there's Avery better known as Demon, and the baby Asher also known as Wicked."

She nodded to everyone as I went down the line. "It's nice to meet everyone. Isn't there a rule about calling you by club name only? The clubs in Brazil insisted we call them by their club name...or else. They weren't so forgiving even if you were a woman." She rubbed her hands nervously which caused me to squeeze her tighter for reassurance, to let her know she was safe.

Lucifer sat at the head of the table, "Well, we're not neanderthal brutes like them; the club name rule only applies to the bunnies. From what I can see, you're on your way to ol' lady status. Eventually, we hope you'll consider us family."

A tear falls and I wipe it away, kissing her temple then helped her sit at the table, wrapping my arm over the top of her chair.

"Aww, I knew it!" A tiny yet mighty voice came from the kitchen and in walks Lila.

"Lil, long time no see."

She stood beside me, squeezing my shoulders and giving me a half hug. "Yeah, that's what happens when you're in love. You know what I mean, don't you?" She raises her brow and I chuckle. "Lila, this is Avi. Avi, the one I told you about." I spin my finger near my temple, calling her crazy and she punches my arm before extending her hand to Avi.

"It's nice to finally meet the girl who stole his heart. If you need any X-rated dirt..." She winked and Avi laughed. "We'll definitely talk later!" And they giggle like schoolgirls.

Oh brother.

Then my little tater tot comes out with a platter full of pancakes with Sam carrying the bacon and eggs. Sam then goes back and retrieves biscuits and gravy, her old man's favorite. He growls while pulling her into his lap; she squeals, "Not in front of children."

Now that's a first said within these walls. He whispered something in her ear and she shoved him and sat in the chair beside him.

Raven sits on her knees, grabs a plate, and hands it to her mother, me, and then herself. She picks two blueberry pancakes and a chocolate chip, puts a piece of bacon and some egg on each, pours the syrup, rolls it up, and eats it.

"That was a very smart idea, tater tot. Where did you learn that from?"

"Mommy's friend, Diesel, taught me. He taught me lots of fun food stuff and he liked playing with me outside. He was nice. I miss him, *mamae*." Her face fell and her mother rubbed her cheek, "I know, sweetheart, but he's in heaven and watches over you every day." That made her happy and she returned to eating her breakfast burrito.

I nudge Avi and we lean away from Raven, whispering low, "What happened? Did Frankie kill him?" She nodded, looking up to avoid crying. "Shot him twice, but he was still alive. Then... Frankie shot him point blank. I know where he's buried. I wrote a lot of stuff I remembered to give to the Chief. Can we go talk to him after this?"

Any evidence she had against him would bring us closer to peace. "Sure."

At the station, we wait for someone to gather the information. Chief Grady walks in, "Cullen, Ms. Cabrera, good to see you both. Since you're here, I'll be the bearer of bad news. You'll have to testify in court next week, Avi. Frankie's case is being expedited so he can be tried in Brazil. With enough evidence on our end, we can have him sentenced to a South American maximum-security prison for the rest of his life."

"That sounds like great news! I can finally be rid of my brother."

Chief looks at me and I feel the dread coming, her part in this had great news but mine...

"I'm sorry, I tried to get them to drop the criminal charges of accessories and drug trafficking but it's a no-go. They're going to bring up charges against you and Frankie is using what he knows about you guys to cop a plea deal."

"WHAT?!" Avi sits up in her chair scraping the floor. "He's just trying to take everyone down. He's the criminal, not them! You have to keep trying!"

"You're also included, he tipped off child protective services about your daughter but there's nothing they can do since you aren't a US citizen but they called Immigration. I sent your amnesty paperwork high priority so we're at a standstill for now."

I knew he'd throw us under the bus but to call child protective services on your sister is low even for him.

"We need every piece of information to strengthen this case. You said you had critical information for me?"

She straightens up against her chair, leaning against the table.

"No."

Chapter Thirty-Six
Avi

"No."

"Avi, what are you doing?!"

"Chief, I have critical information that will seal the deal on my brother. More than what I already told you. I will exchange all I know for immunity to keep the Merciless Few from persecution."

I lean back in confidence but I can see Cullen is about to lose his shit. He's looking dead at me but I continue to look ahead.

"Avi, you can't do this! You have to tell him. We can handle a little jail time. You and the girls will be safe, that's all that matters."

"NO! After all he's done to you... to me and my little girl! If I can't have him dead, then locked away is the next best thing. Do we have a deal?"

They both think I'm nuts but I'm the only one that can lead them to Diesel's body and probably more. He probably has his own personal cemetery. They should excavate his entire yard. Who knows how many migrant workers died at Frankie's hands?! But not until I am guaranteed that my new family is safe.

"Ms. Cabrera, how do I know I can trust you to deliver?"

"Have I not done so already? Just because I'm working drugs out of my system thanks to that *cadela* doesn't mean I have forgotten every single hellish second in that house. Do you know he threatened to do vile, despicable things to me, his sister?! At one point, I thought...he would..."

I couldn't even finish, I felt so nauseous and dry-heaved. Wondering if I could make it to a receptacle in time.

"I want him to burn in hell for the trauma he caused my daughter and me. I assure you with this evidence you'll never have to worry about Frankie Cabrera again, but NOT until they have immunity."

I stood a bit shaky from revealing one of the dark moments that Cullen didn't know about. His silence spoke volumes. He was seething on the inside; he would gladly go to prison for Frankie's murder but I have to prevent all of that. We have to do this the right way. For my happiness, I DESERVE my happiness with him and my baby girl.

The Chief sighs and leans forward, "You have my word that I will try, Ms. Cabrera. Cullen, I will talk to Rocco about strategy."

"And I will give you a handwritten, signed statement of what I know. Everything, including what I already told you. A side question for you, have you completed searching his house? I'd like to gather my belongings if I can."

"Yes, we completed it two days ago. Anything in that house that is your property you can collect."

"Thank you. Come on, let's go." I walk out with an infuriated biker behind me. He wants to yell and tell me I am crazy, that he is fine doing time for his transactions for Frankie, but I refuse to let that happen.

Frankie is the one who set foot in this country and decided not to improve it but to tear it down with drugs; he chose to trap and coerce girls to work and degrade themselves to make him money, forcing the migrant workers to work in his drug houses to cook and distribute his drugs, he chose to pull the trigger to kill the only man who cared for me before Cullen so no, I will not bend so that there is an iota of a chance for his release.

We get in the truck, and he slams the door harder than need be, making me flinch and he shifts to face me. I hesitated for as long as I could before I looked at a man who felt helpless.

"Why didn't you tell me? That he... I..." His voice changed; it was wracked with hurt. Pain, he couldn't save me from.

"I didn't want you to look at me differently if I told you I thought my brother was going to assault me. The mental, verbal, and even physical abuse I could tell you every moment second to second, but I only remember bits and pieces of the incident. I never want to relive those moments. I never want to feel that type of fear again!"

He pulls me toward him, I try to look out the window, but his fingers pull my face in his direction. "You may have to bring it up in court. I will never understand what you went through, but I'll be there when you do. Okay?"

I didn't expect to cry but the tears fell so easily as our foreheads touched and he squeezed my cheeks, getting me to laugh through my tears.

"I'm so sorry I wasn't there." He felt so guilty for something he couldn't predict. Nobody could have.

"How could you have known? If you had I know you would have been my knight in shining armor like you are now." I break the hold and wipe my tears, "Now can we go and get my stuff?"

"Yeah. Are you sure about this deal? What if it doesn't work like you want?"

"At least I tried instead of standing by watching you go

down with Frankie. I deserve my happiness...and that's with you."

He kisses my hand and starts the truck. When we arrive, there is police tape everywhere, but I see the area where Diesel is buried is still untouched, for now. I maneuver under the tape with the help of my cane and he follows behind me. The place looks like it was hit by a tornado with no effort to put anything back. I head towards my room and as expected, it mirrored what the rest of the house looked like. I was able to salvage most of our clothes, her purple blanket, and Theodore, her teddy bear. The other teddy bear I stashed my earnings was lying on the bed. I pulled out the money and he looked shocked.

"Guess we can put this in your account?" I go into the bathroom to grab her favorite bubble bath and my perfume. I was able to pack everything into a duffle bag, almost less than what I came here with, but I've gained so much more than material things.

I'm happy with what I have.

Chapter Thirty-Seven
Reaper

She's completely batshit crazy. Holding onto damning proof to make sure we all go scot-free? I could yell at her until my ears bleed, but she won't waver. I've got to let this play out.

After gathering her things, we return and she decides to take a nap, Raven curls up beside her, and I can't help but smile at how beautiful my girls are but frown at all they've gone through.

I go back to the living room after closing the door quietly. I gathered everyone in the living room, I relayed what went down since we left.

"Wow, I can't even imagine. Not from my own brother. He's a vile, despicable monster!" Sam's eyes fill with angry tears. She wipes them away as Lucifer tries to comfort her while equally as infuriated as I am.

"She says she has more evidence that would take Frankie down but..." I look around to see the concern. "Not until they find a way to get us off, cleared of all charges."

"What?! Is she mad?! She needs to tell them! You have to make her tell them! We're not afraid of doing time. We need to put the final nail in Frankie's coffin." Fiend tries to whisper but judging by the door creak he failed.

"And I will..." We turn to see Avi slowly making her way to the sofa without her cane. "I want nothing more than to never see or hear his name again. What I know is vital but so is having you all in my life. That little girl in there adores each and every one of you. You are the family she deserves and I'm going to do my damndest to give it to her."

Everyone is speechless.

"I'm sorry, but please trust me on this. I can at least try."

Lucifer puffs his cigar, "We really don't have a choice. Thank you for thinking of us as family."

Then we hear tiny feet shuffling, so much for nap time. Sam jumps up, "Since there's time before dinner how about we set up the new pool for a special little girl. Gee, I wonder where she could be?!"

"Here I am! I want to go swimming, can I *mamae*, I mean momma?"

"Of course, I got your clothes and purpie blanket from the house. Your bathing suit should be in there, too. We'll be out there a bit later, okay? You listen to what Miss Sam says." She didn't even answer, just squealed, found her suit, and changed in the common bathroom.

Avi grabbed my face and my attention. I leaned down for a kiss and realized it was a very public display of affection when I leaned back. Something I never did even when Daisy tried to force my hand to establish superiority amongst the bunnies.

Avi blushes when she realizes everyone is around and I swear I hear Lil giggling in the background.

Avi stands and holds out her hand. "Come on, I need your help...umm, unpacking since we'll be cramming our stuff with yours."

I see Sam smirk as everyone piles out of the house.

"No problem. I got room in my closet because I wear t-shirts most of the time and those can be shoved into a drawer and give you the rest of the space. Long as you don't mind sharing the underwear drawer with me?"

"As long as you can differentiate my pretty little thongs from your boxers in the dark, we should be fine."

I shuddered to think how often I'll get to touch the delicate fabric that lay against her soft skin and sweetness.

Chapter Thirty-Eight
Avi

Raven could play for hours outside in that pool they got for her. The guys turned on some music and fired up the grill. I think Sam understood my nonverbal plea. The house was empty for now.

"Come on then, no time like the present." I pull him up by his scarred arm, which he wraps around me. I wonder just how long it'll take for it to look normal or if it will heal completely. We walk in tandem as he attacks my neck while I lead the way.

Little did he know he was only fueling the flames.

I wouldn't wait another minute.

I needed him.

My body begged for his touch, to feel his raw emotion for me. A physical bond between a man and a woman because although I am confident in my testimony, I may never get this chance again if I am wrong. I couldn't bear never feeling the intimate touch of his strong hands if they sent him to prison, even if only for this one day.

He separates from me to pull all his shirts from the second

drawer and shove them into the bottom one. He then opens the top to slide all his underwear to one side. He had more pairs than I thought the average guy would have.

"I'll make room in the closet while you put your stuff away. I should have some extra hangers in here somewhere; if not I'm sure someone does." He has a deep closet so he steps in and I can hear him moving things around.

I pull off my sandals and plant my feet firmly and peel everything off while leaning against the dresser with one leg bent, resting on the lip of the bottom drawer. I felt my skin flush and my body warm as I wait anxiously for him to come out. I felt breathless in anticipation.

What if he wasn't ready for that yet? Was I rushing this? Guess I would find out because there was no going back.

I wanted this. I wanted him.

"Everything okay out there?" His deep voice caused goosebumps all over. I could have climaxed from that alone; I was so worked up.

I cleared my throat to sound confident even though I wasn't. "Umm, I could use some help."

His hand appears first with a bunch of clothes on hangers and then he steps out, immediately dropping everything.

I should have never doubted a thing. He growled as he took in the sight of my naked curves. The desire that radiated between us was undeniable. He was going to ravage me.

"Av-Avi..." His chest rose and fell with rapid breaths, nothing sexier than a man trying to maintain his cool.

I give him a seductive smirk while I twirled a piece of my hair around my finger. He tries to form a coherent sentence.

"Damn..." He scratched his goatee as he stepped forward but I held my hand up.

"Stop. Take everything off. I want to see if my wet dream even comes close to the real thing. Is this what you expected?"

He slips off his shirt and I see the extent of his road rash in the front. It still looked pretty wicked even though it was healing. That doesn't stop him from looking appetizing.

A deep laugh slips his lip, "I don't think my imagination even came close to creating something so absolutely beautiful. What about everyone else?"

I slide my finger from my collarbone down between my breasts. "I'm pretty confident Sam got my subtle hint earlier. Besides, if you hurry it won't be an issue."

He unzips his jeans to reveal he isn't wearing underwear. Now there's only space between us which he closed immediately and now I'm wrapped around his waist, rubbing against him to get the slightest bit of relief while I shove my tongue down his throat. Or was it the other way around? I didn't care. "I've never rushed this moment in my fantasies and I'm damn sure not going to in real life. I've waited for far too long."

He tosses me on his bed, our bed, I suppose. He makes sure the door is closed and then locks it to avoid a parent's biggest fear.

I watched him stalk me, slowly, methodically. His strong, callused hands uncrossed my legs, sliding up my ankles upward followed by the warmth of his lips. His touch felt like sparks against my skin creating a chain reaction. I tried to bite back a scream, slapping my hand over my mouth, but he bit the sensitive part of my inner thigh causing me to whimper and writhe to get away from him but he just drags me back to his face. His breath relentlessly torturing me. "Cullen, please... I can't keep quiet if you keep doing that." After pleading, I cover my mouth again to muffle the moan threatening to roar forward.

"No point in trying, darlin'. I'm sure everyone knows that her parents are indulging in much-needed adult activities. They'll keep her as busy as I'll keep you with endless orgasms.

Now, keep those legs open, darlin' or I'll be forced to give you another love bite."

I heard his instruction, but it was what he said prior that made me sit up. I looked down at the man who spoke the sweetest words I had ever heard.

"H-her parents? Really?"

He nibbled closer to my spot while simultaneously using his fingers to tease me. "You heard what I said. I claimed her, I can be her father, Avi. Only if you let me." This time he pushed my knee down so he could gain better access and further drive me wild.

I tried to sit up and rock against him, but his relentless teasing felt like punishment, as he refused to let me cum all over his lips and fingertips. I was pouting until his large hand slapped my inner thigh causing a painfully delicious sting.

That's going to leave a big mark.

He hovers over me, kissing me slowly, and lovingly as he works his way back down. He's revving me up like the engine on his bike. "There...please...don't stop." I huff when he stops moving his fingers but gasp when he devours me.

"Oh God!" Was all I could spit out before trying to muffle my screams with a pillow. He snatches it away, shaking his head. I tried to reason with him, but my body surrenders to the pleasure. I felt the knot tighten before it snapped like a rubber band.

"Mmmmphhhh....fuck me! God!" My legs shook and my body shuddered as I clamped down on him. He didn't seem to mind; in fact, he was laughing and the motion tickled my now sensitive clit. I open my legs and stare down at him. "Is that my new pet name, darlin'? Babe, Mr. Wonderful, or stud muffin will do." I couldn't help but laugh.

I pull and flip him so I'm straddling him, his dick pressed against my stomach. I think he was fully hard or at least I hoped so because I was already concerned about what was in front of me.

Mas minha mãe não criou nenhuma cadela. (but my mama didn't raise no bitch)

I leaned forward, "Ok, stud muffin..." He leaned up for a kiss but I had already started sliding away from his lips to lay against him while gripping his dick. I could barely wrap my fingers around it. I see his body jerk to the touch as I slow stroke him.

"Oh baby, shit. Keep doing that and I'm going to blow my load." He leans forward enough to smack and squeeze my ass, sure to have left his mark once again.

"Well then, we'll be even. One orgasm each." I lick the tip. I wondered... could I fit him in my mouth? The answer to that was almost and that was the best kind of problem to have. His hand lay on my head, not shoving me down but there to show how much he was enjoying it, although his moans were a dead giveaway. A man moaning is the sexiest thing alive. It means he's comfortable letting his guard down and expressing emotion. I hum to his moaning which vibrates against him. "Holy fuck, Avi." He quickly pulls me up against him, side by side. I rock against him to feel any semblance of friction, "I need you..."

He kisses me enough to distract me from him slowly filling me to the brim. I gasped into our kiss. When he couldn't fill me any further, he stilled himself but I could feel him pulsing against my walls. He grunts and grits his teeth, "Baby... oh baby, you're as tight as a vice grip. Ride me."

He shifts and I turn to face him. Easing myself down, panting as he fills me up once more. He exhales hard this time, placing his hands on my waist, coaxing me back and forth until I take over. I speed up when I feel his thumb circling my clit. It went from feeling good to a warmth that covered me warning me of my impending orgasm. I rock harder and faster. "K-keep going! I'm going to cum! I'm going to..." I couldn't finish my sentence before I was shaking all over him, squeezing him even tighter.

He slammed upward trying to chase down his release. "Oh, baby, you take me so well. I'm so close...so fucking...close..." He laced our fingers together as I rocked harder back and forth, up and down. He slid his hands up to squeeze my nipples, a super sensitive area that set off a surprise orgasm. "Let it go, Avi. I want to feel you shatter all over my cock, baby." He grunted his release as I collapsed on his chest.

He kissed my forehead as I lightly touched the road rash and his body shook. "Ooh, I don't know why that tingles, but I like it. You okay?" He brushes my hair out of my face and I half-smile. "Yeah, of course. I initiated this. No regrets except now we'll have to get creative with Raven around."

"Oh, there are plenty of options, the bathroom, the garage, we can hop on my bike."

"You've thought about this, haven't you?"

"A little."

"Maybe we'll try that bathroom idea after she's gone to bed tonight?" I graze his scars and notice that it causes his dick to thump against his stomach. "Stop that, or we won't leave this room."

I slide off of him and sit on the edge, stretching. I look back to see him grinning. "You're such a perv."

"Wait a minute, you seduced me, remember?" I didn't reply but instead went to the dresser and put on my red high-cut two-piece bathing suit. He was in front of me so quick, it wasn't too hard to figure out what he was thinking.

"Not a chance, Avi." He was ready to slip a sack over my head until I pushed him back on the bed and straddled him again, his hands automatically on my hips. "This is the tamest swimsuit I own unless you want me to wear one of my thongs. You know Brazil is known for the thong bikini. Besides, you've made your mark on me, quite literally. Everybody will know that I'm yours." I opened my legs slightly to show his teeth marks on my inner thighs and the slap mark and I'm pretty sure there are fingerprints on my hips, tits, and ass.

He growled, "Damn right you're mine." He changes into some board shorts and follows me out of the room.

As we walk through the house toward the front door, Lila saunters out of the kitchen with a huge smile on her face while sipping on something in a mason jar.

"I hope I taught you well...sounds like I did." She points down to his markings on my legs. I groan while looking at him in that 'I told you so' look.

"Shut up, Lil."

She stands in front of him looking up, strong in her stance despite her tiny stature. "Tell me I'm wrong? Avi?"

There's a story, but later for that, we girls will have a chat soon. She may know some tricks I can use. He can't have all the mind-blowing moves. She sized him up with her brow raised and I concede, shrugging my shoulders, "Well, she's not wrong."

"HA! I knew it. High five girl!" Her mouth curved into a smile as she slaps me five. He stays quiet as he pulls me outside.

I see my little girl splashing around in this rectangular pool, big enough for kids but somehow Demon wedged himself in there with her, squirting her with his water gun. Fiend tosses in water balloons that she throws to the best of her ability. Her squeals and laughing is music to my ears. This is the first time I've seen her genuinely happy in such a long time.

I can't let Frankie take this from her. This is her family now. She has a man who lovingly claims her as his own. No, I was going to make sure Frankie goes down on his own.

Later that day, I look up at him as I lay against him in the lounger. I was watching Raven like a hawk. It'll be hard for me to relinquish some of this control, but I know I don't have to raise her alone. She's got us.

"Hey..." He catches my attention, so I look up at him, "she's fine. You've got to relax."

"You've got to understand, it's only been a few days; it's going to take time. Everything is new, I'm trying to relax but every time I did something bad would happen. But...I'm glad to do this with you." I tilt my head up for a kiss and he obliges.

"EWWWW! *Mamae*, boys have dirty, icky cooties!" He frowns but I chuckle, "Who told you that?"

"Marissa! She said boy cooties make you sick."

Now he looks at me for clarification, "Marissa was one of the girls on the boat. I swear she soaks everything up."

I watch her run around and then splash into the pool. "Cullen?"

"Yeah?"

"Are you happy with this sudden shift? I feel like a burden, that you feel obligated to and I want you to know that you aren't. I don't want you to feel trapped."

He takes my hand, threading our fingers together before kissing each of my fingers. "Trapped? Nothing could be farther from the truth. It's you that is my saving grace. After all I've been through, meeting you was the stability I needed. Guess stability isn't the correct word, but it showed that my problems are small in comparison. So, what if I went through a bad breakup because she cheated? There are worse things."

"Well, you got pretty banged up, so I think that is significant and compound it with her sleazing it up with Frankie. Everything happened for you to find me. For you to save me; I'll be forever grateful for that. And now, you want to raise Raven. I couldn't ask for more. This is enough and I'm not going to let *aquele bastardo* (that bastard) take you guys away from us."

"I know what that means. Shhh," He kisses my forehead where it was wrinkled in frustration, "no more talk of him."

"Mama! Come swim with me!"

"Alright, sweetie."

For the next week, I wrote an entire thesis about my time with Frankie, how he operated and where he stashed his product and money. He didn't have a checking account as an illegal alien, but he had two safes in the house. One behind his desk in the wall and the other behind a huge portrait in the hallway on his side of the house. I knew he kept a list of clients and if they didn't have it already, I bet my life it was in the safe probably along with other damning evidence.

Lastly, I gave the exact location of where he crudely buried Diesel and suggested they excavate the entire yard for other victims. I didn't want to let on, but I was terrified to testify in court. I know he couldn't hurt me anymore but reliving everything will be emotionally damaging. I didn't want Cullen to have to deal with trying to build me up from ruin, but I needed to do this...for her. Maybe one day I'll be able to afford counseling for both of us.

Three days later, the time had come. Everyone was adamant about getting up and dressed to accompany me to court. I asked Lila and the girls to watch Raven; no way was I going to let her relive another gut-wrenching moment. I'll gladly take her to the station if they need her testimony.

knock knock

I'm knocked out of my thoughts, "Avi, you ready?"

"Why are you knocking? It's your room."

"It's OUR room but I didn't know if you needed a moment to yourself. This is big, testifying against your family."

"He is NOT *mi familia! Para o inferno com ele!*" (*to hell with him*)

He pulls me to him, hugging me but staying quiet. I can feel my anger subside. I look into his eyes as he gazes into mine. I sighed long and hard, "Thank you, sweetheart. Let's get this over with."

Chapter Thirty-Nine
Reaper

She hasn't stopped shaking her leg since we sat down in the courtroom. I place my hand on it and she immediately stops. Her jaw was clenched as she grinded her teeth as a coping mechanism.

"Sorry." I take her hand and kiss it, causing her face to relax. "You can do this, baby. I'm so proud of you."

"All rise!"

We stand for the judge's entrance into the courtroom and get ready for the longest day or days of our lives. They started with the detectives on the case and their findings. Examining and cross-examining only lasted about 90 minutes; the defense never stood a chance.

Once that part was done, the attorney started calling character witnesses, starting strong with her. Avi stood up and walked confidently to the stand, repeating the oath before she sat down all while keeping her focus on me. She recalled everything she remembered, confidently answering the rebuttal questions, and never wavering in her purpose to send Frankie to prison for the rest of his life. Nothing could deter her, not even his sneers from behind the table. No doubt he was trying to intimidate and scare her into submission. I wanted nothing more than to pummel his face until I felt his skull crack and even that wouldn't stop me.

The defense lawyer really tried to take her down with him as a willing accomplice, but she had an answer for everything that pointed towards forced labor.

"Admit it, Ms. Cabrera, you willingly helped your brother distribute and sell drugs. You wanted a better life for your child and now, you'll say anything to stay out of jail."

I could see she wanted to act emotionally but then she closed her eyes, took in a deep breath, then calmly responded. "Do you have children, Mr. Philipps? I can tell that you do not. A parent will do whatever it takes for their child but that is a different story when you are being threatened to have your child taken away. I don't know U.S. law well enough, but I feared he could have her taken away or worse. He threatened to kill my daughter! His own flesh and blood and until you feel the absolute fear of losing your only child, I would not expect you to understand, Mr. Philipps. I did not willingly do anything. He promised to take care of us and when I refused to be a prostitute, he forced my hand. I have here a 22-page report of everything that happened during my time there. I sent copies to the Chief of Police, DOJ, and ICE in case something mysteriously happened to this copy that will be put on record." She also gave a copy to us to lock away in our safe. She didn't know how far Frankie's reach was, but she was taking no chances.

The prosecution stands up, "And tell us, Ms. Cabrera, what makes this manifesto different from what you said during the investigation?"

"I made sure to recall everything single low-down, filthy, vile detail. Including vital information of the location of his murdered bodyguard Hershel! I witnessed it! He could have survived but Frankie shot him point blank in the chest and had him buried near the tree line on the west side of the house. He probably executed more people, immigrants who only wanted a better life. You can't report them missing because according to law they were illegal and basically didn't exist! He's a goddamned murderer and I'll have nightmares of every single day I spent in the presence of the devil himself." She sneered.

Frankie shot up, trying to lunge over the table but didn't make it far with the police right behind him.

"*Eu vou the mater, sua vadia estupida! Você está morto para mim!* Do you hear me, Avi!" (I'm going to kill you, you stupid bitch! You're dead to me!) He snarled as they tried to get him to settle down.

My Portuguese wasn't that good to decipher but I see the effect it has on her. She flinched, her face paled, and the confidence she once had was replaced by fear and heartbreak. He was her brother and that kind of pain hurts the most. I shot up almost after he did to protect her if I had to, but the brothers held me in place.

"Order in the court, everybody! Get a rein on your client, I will not tolerate another outburst from anyone in this courtroom! I will clear it out! Ms. Cabrera, you may step down. The court is in recess for one hour, dismissed!" He slams down his gavel and everyone starts to exit.

Avi stepped down off the stand and she looked unstable as she clutched her stomach. She bee-lined it out of the courtroom. I followed her as fast as I could. I see her turn into the bathroom and then, unfortunately, I could hear her. I didn't hesitate to go right in behind her, this was an emergency, the other women would just have to understand. She was in the stall, collapsed on the floor emptying her stomach violently.

I opened the partially closed door and held her hair while

she cried and heaved. Whatever he said had shaken her to the core. She bawled profusely, laying her head on the seat.

I flush the toilet and pull her up, she leaned against me for strength after vomiting so violently. "Come on, sweetie. Let's wash up and go home. You did your job; I don't want you here."

She looked at her mascara smeared face and cried harder. I pulled her into me and let her cry onto my shirt. I leaned against the sink rubbing her back and whispering how brave I thought she was and how much I cared.

A few minutes later she leans back sniffling. "Oh, your shirt. I ruined it." She tries to wipe it. "I couldn't care less. I'm more worried about you. Can you tell me what he said? My Portuguese isn't that good but I saw your whole demeanor change."

"It's not only what he said; it's the fact that he was so willing to toss me under the bus and estrange himself from the only family he had left. I know this sounds crazy, but up until that minute, I was willing to visit him if they sentenced and kept him here. He was still *mi familia*, (my family) you know? You don't turn your back; you try to help no matter how angry you are. And now, he wished me dead. Said I was dead to him and it was too much. And the worst part is if I hadn't thought quickly, he probably would have at the hospital. Why do I still love the man who wants to kill me? He used to be my brother! My brother..."

I didn't have an answer for her, but I understood her frustration. Forget all the stuff done to me and our feud, he was supposed to be the salvation to her awful life back home, but he ended up treating her worse.

"Hey, look at me. No matter what he says or what happens, you have me. You have a whole family who only wants to see you grow. Do you want to stay and see this through or go home?"

"We can't go back in there Cullen, your shirt."

"Who cares. I'm your support through this."

She wipes her face and exhales her frustration. "I want to see this through."

We walked out to a few stares because this did not look as innocent as it was. I take her hand and we find the group. Sam looks concerned, "Hey sweetie, you, okay?"

Her eyes filled with tears, "My brother wished me dead; it's heartbreaking and relieving at the same time. I shouldn't be so upset but..."

"But nothing. He's still your brother and that's one of the most hurtful things you could say."

"It hurts more than I thought it would, but I'll be okay." Sam wraps her up in a motherly hug and kisses her forehead. "That's right. You will be okay. Let's walk the block before court is back in session. Some girl time and fresh air. Is that okay?" She looks at me, "Of course." Before she's out of my view, she gives me a small smile.

I rub my face and groan loudly before sitting down on a bench. I feel a pat on my back and look to see Lucifer. "I've never seen someone so heartbroken, boss. She physically purged her pain and all I could do was hold her hair. I never want to see her that distraught ever again. But...what if we do get prison time? Sometimes I wonder if I really am what she needs. I don't have a job; I'm living essentially at home and have no real goals besides hopping on my bike. How can I support them with that?"

"Son, all of this just happened, everything piled up at once and you're feeling the pressure; that's okay. Baby steps, no one expects you to put on a suit, buy a car and a house, and work at the bank. If you want to find steady employment, do that. If you want to find a space more tailored for you and them; we're behind you 100%, but don't you dare think about pulling away from them. She loves you..."

I hear the word echo...*love*. She hadn't said it but I felt it.

"And all this worry about your stability and being able to provide for them is your version of love. You two may not even have said it but you're displaying your love language."

My eyebrow shot up. "What do you know about that?"

"The missus made me read it, literally plopped in my lap and read it together. At first, I was annoyed but then I really got to learn what makes her happy and she learned what I enjoy. We've never been happier. Being a biker is a part of me; I'm a husband and a grandfather now. Labels, Reap, they're labels. You have labels, too. Take it one day at a time and know that you'll always have your brothers behind you no matter what you do."

He leaves me to my thoughts; I had the perfect endgame in mind, but it would take some work to get there.

IF I avoid jail time.

Chapter Forty
Avi

The warmth of the sun on my face and the fresh air was what I needed to get away from the room full of misery.

I was so awestruck by the man who held my hair, who picked me up off the floor and held me while I broke down. Then he put my fragile pieces together and I couldn't ask for more. I never prayed so hard to get my happily ever after. I wanted this to be over already.

Sam's hug wraps me in the warmth of genuine love. "Avi, I would never tell Cullen this, but there's not a day I don't constantly pray that he finds a wife and creates a family. Each of my boys are different; some will never fall in love or settle down, but I know that settling down is ideal for my sweet boy."

"That's so sweet, but I don't want to take him from his family."

"You are not taking *him* from *us*. We're adding *you* to our family."

I felt a lump in my throat as I expressed my worst fear. "Sam, what if they get sent to prison?"

Sam slows her steps, "Rocco and I have talked about this

extensively and if it comes down to that, I hope it's minimal. I would visit the man I love every weekend while still tending to club business. He taught me everything including telling me that he has stashed a year's worth of funds in the bank for expenses. He's always had a plan B for whatever the case may be. You, me, and the girls will be okay. Let's be optimistic, especially with the situation you just came out of. Come on, before they lock us out of the courtroom."

When we pass the double doors of the entrance, I see them talking to the Chief.

Oh no.

Chapter Forty-One
Reaper

Speaking of avoiding jail time, the Chief pulls us to the side. "Rocco, boys. I have an update for you. Let's play a game of good news, bad news..."

Court has reconvened and Avi is back on the stand giving the remainder of her testimony. This time she seems more confident and not concerned about Frankie's sneers or intimidation tactics. I honestly don't think I'd be quite as calm if I knew about everything outside of the trial beforehand.

"Ms. Cabrera, thank you for your time and for your written statement." She nods and steps off the stand and sits right next to me. Her body relaxes into me as I squeeze her hand, staring daggers at Frankie as I kiss her temple. "I'm so proud of you, darlin'." She squeezes me back.

I couldn't wait to get home, to spend some alone time together in peace and silence. Court adjourned for the day and would resume sometime next week. We walk out hand in hand. "What a day. I just want to fall asleep between you and Raven."

"Yeah well, I might have a surprise for you at home. I asked the girls to take Raven to the nearby pond and park for a few hours."

"You did? What are you up to?"

"Let's get back and I'll show you. Don't worry; she ate before they left and they're bringing snacks and a change of clothes. Lila's become her best friend. I think it's because they're the same size."

"Ooh don't repeat that in her presence. She looks like a scrapper and I'm not fighting for you."

I poke her side and she squeals, "Not even going to help your man?" She shakes her head laughing as she tries to walk ahead but I pull her against me as we head to the parking lot.

Today, I introduced Avi to my Betty girl. Feeling Avi squeeze me as we hit a straightaway going 70+ mph or when we take a curve was the best. I loved this feeling of my favorite girl against me while riding on my second favorite girl. Betty girl understood her taking second place in my life, but I'd never leave her.

Finally, we got home and I led her to our bathroom. I run the water and add the soap. I set my speaker up, play some calming music, and pull her towards me. I placed my lips on hers, softly at first, but then she pulled at my hair and I tightened my grip around her waist, about to lose control.

"Avi, I'm on a hair trigger."

She smiles; it's not a normal smile; it's a mischievous one. She allows me to finish preparing the bath, set up the towels, and light a few candles while she waits on the bed. I could take her there too, rip off her clothes not giving her enough time to respond before I have her cumming all over my fingers first.

Stick to the plan.

I stand in front of her and slowly peel off my shirt. Her eyes are low and filled with wanting. Begging me to fulfill every sexual fantasy that's been playing in her head since we met.

Now her delicate hands are on my chest. Her nails rake down causing a bolt of electricity from my spine to my balls. I kiss her and when I separate, she places her finger on my lips, I kiss it in reply.

"I want you to strip me naked."

She didn't have to say another word as I started with her blouse, unbuttoning it to reveal a sheer bra, my hands immediately covering her as she gasped to the warmth. I see her reach behind and undo the bra, which falls into my hands. I let it fall so I could feel her soft breasts and hardened nipples. Pinching them because I know how much it riles her up. I surprise her by turning her so her back was against my chest, wrapping one hand around her neck while the other trailed between her breasts to the button of her pants. I was able to unbutton it with one hand while squeezing the other. Her response was to clench her legs together, but I tapped her pussy lightly outside of her matching sheer panties, allowing her no protection against my hand. "Don't try to keep me from what's mine." I warn her.

"Oh! Mmm...more..." She whispered, her hands now trying to guide me between her legs; I could feel the heat radiating from her. At this point, we'd never make it into the tub. I slid my fingers underneath the underwear and she froze; only her labored breathing was heard. I kiss her neck, "Patience. Hop in the tub." She looked disappointed as she slid into the warm sudsy water. I rip everything off and slip in behind her. I wrap my arm around her shoulders while opening her legs. She exhales as the warm water teases her alongside my fingers. Lightly brushing against her as she tries to beg for more friction.

"Stop teasing. You wouldn't like it if I..." Her hand slipped behind her, her fingertips stroking my dick, but I wanted to feel her whole hand and more. Done with the teasing, I tell her to turn around and she straddles me. I graze her lips with my finger, then roughly grab the back of her neck, taking advantage of her gasp by slamming her lips onto mine at the same time she slips down on my cock. Both of us let out a mutual moan.

"Fuck, baby girl. I want to spend all night feeling you climax all over me. To have you screaming my name over and over again until you tap out."

My words seem to motivate her as she rocks against me, harder and faster, "Cull-Cullen! Yes...yes! I'm gonna...ohhh..." She lets out this ear-piercing scream that turns into a moan as she slumps against me. I pumped against her, gripping her hips as I slammed her down on me. It seemed to revive her as she grinds against me, but this time to get me to cum.

"You're so hard. I can feel you getting harder. Cum for me, I want to feel you." The water sloshes around as she ups the tempo again. Back and forth, up and down, I couldn't predict her movement, only enjoying the freight train that was barreling ahead to an explosive end.

"Avi, yes baby, there!" I smacked her ass hard and I swear she came all over me again. She was even tighter and wetter. "Oh Avi...ahhh!" She shrieked as I lurched upward then she giggled as I sank back down in the tub, panting like I ran a marathon. I rub her back and she kisses me gently.

"Mmm, I love your kisses, darlin'."

Chapter Forty-Two
Avi

Bliss, total and complete bliss as I lay against the man who protects me and gives me peace. His touch is comforting like I don't have to be on the defensive, that I can relax.

"Avi, baby, we need to talk."

I lean back with my brow raised, "Are you breaking up with me? That's how this sounds, like break-up sex."

He laughs but I'm not. "No, I'm never letting you go, I told you that and I meant it. I got some news earlier today and I didn't know when the right time was to tell you. It's a bit of a good news and bad news situation."

Now my anxiety is intensified; not only does he want to "talk" but it's the old good news/bad news bit. Right after mind-blowing sex.

"Ugh, give me the bad news first."

"Do you want to get out of the tub first?"

"Don't you dare try to change the subject!" I could feel the tears forming. He wipes away a rogue tear before he taps my chin.

"Thanks to your testimony, and the discovery of the bodies

like you said, it looks like they have more than enough to extradite Frankie back to South America and set him up in the most fortified prison. He'll spend his sentence in solitary confinement."

Well, that sounded like great news!

"But..."

Ahh, there it is...

"We can't avoid charges but they were downgraded and we'll only spend six months in prison."

"WHAT?! Six months! What can I do? What do I tell Raven? How will I...I... no, I can't do this without you!" I was crying so hard I was shaking.

"I told you, you, Sam, and the girls will be taken care of. We'll make sure of it. Yes, it breaks my heart to leave you but if we hadn't taken the plea deal, we were facing ten plus years and I'd go crazy."

I can feel myself hyperventilating as he pulls the drain from the tub and dries us off. I slip into his shirt and a pair of my shorts, we're in complete silence and it's deafening. I'm trying to prolong talking about this further. I'm folding my t-shirts and placing them in the dresser and he figured it out, "Avi, you can't avoid this. It's a done deal, I never wanted to leave you like this, but I'd rather take the deal than chance it." I clench a shirt and then slam it down against the dresser as I drop my head.

"This was supposed to be my vindication! My happy ending, my little girl was going to get the family she deserved. I'm...so...angry!"

He grabs my shoulders and leans against me. I shake my head as I let the tears fall. "We broke the law and this is our punishment. I'll spend every day of my time thinking about the woman whose smart mouth and sweet little girl stole my heart. How I became a protector and companion in a snap of my fingers, how all my past troubles seem worth it because I have you two. This will not break us, Avi. I need you to be strong for me. Look at me..."

I turn around and my heart flutters at the sight of him. What was I going to do? I reluctantly looked him in the eyes. He leans down to kiss me, and it feels like goodbye, making me break down again. He doesn't say anything; he just holds me.

After I don't know how long, we separate. "I'm sorry. I thought everything would be okay, but yet again I was dealt another bad hand. I'm tired of losing, Cullen."

"Baby, this isn't a loss. It's a bump in the road. After this, we start our lives together. Maybe you can start looking at places for us to move into, would you like that? A small house for us and a yard for tater tot to roam in?"

"You're okay with moving out of the clubhouse?"

"Well, darlin' we can't stay crammed in this tiny room. It's time. Oh, I forgot about the good news."

I wasn't feeling too positive after the bad news, but he pulled these two red cards from his wallet and handed it to me.

"U.S. Amnesty card?"

"Yes, they granted you asylum. You don't have to worry about deportation, but you must go through the citizenship process. We'll go to the bookstore and pick up some books on U.S. history. You can take my time away as the opportunity to keep you busy."

And the tears reemerge and I hug him tight, "Oh baby..."

Chapter Forty-Three
Reaper

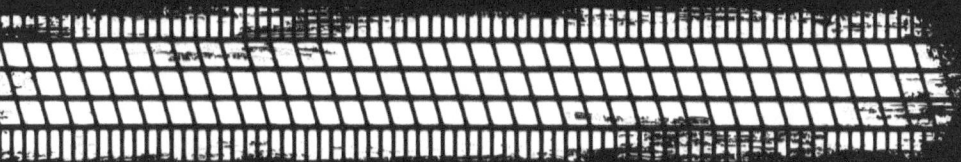

"You can do this. We have to turn ourselves in next week." She gasped and looked away; for her, it was too soon. I hear the front door opening and the tiny footsteps. "Mama, Cullen! I learned to skip rocks!" She shouts as she gets closer to the door; I unlock it. "We can do this together. She's as tough as her mom." I open the door and there she is as happy as can be.

"Hi *mamae*, I skipped rocks!" She repeated and I felt a lump in my throat. Choking down my sadness as I sit next to her and put her on my lap.

"Tater tot, we got to talk to you about something and I want you to be a big girl for me. Can you do that?"

"Uh-huh."

I broke the news gently all while holding her hand. She asked the same questions Avi did and I answered as best I could.

"I know you're sad and it's okay to be sad because I am, too, but I know that when my time is up, I can't wait to see you running into my arms. When we go to the bookstore tomorrow, we'll pick you up some books and a calendar so you can mark off the days, okay? I want you to look after your mom for me."

"I-I don't want you to go! I want you to stay and be my *papai*!" (dad) I was learning every day from her and I understood that clearly.

"Don't worry, I'll always be your *papai*. You're my tater tot. Come here." She leans over and I hug her tightly. I know the circumstances were somber, but I just admitted to being her father, another big step for me as a man.

The three of us spent the afternoon cuddled up in bed. It was bittersweet knowing that by next week I would be in an 8' x 12' cell counting down the seconds until I could make love to Avi again.

When we came out for dinner, the tone was very gloomy. I could tell that Sam had been crying and the girls weren't their usual lively selves.

Lucifer stands, "Look I know this isn't the answer we wanted but it is the lesser of two evils. I have enough money saved for up to a year's worth of bills and utilities. The Merciless chapters from Rhode Island, Connecticut, and New Hampshire will take turns monitoring your safety and checking in. I'll leave all their contact information. They will do rotating one month shifts and the Ace of Spades crew will monitor consistently since they are local. I will be looking for updates. I want to know if anything goes wrong, but I made sure all my girls are going to be safe. Jake and the Aces are coming by tomorrow to introduce themselves and solidify the game plan. I'm sorry that I couldn't get us off completely and that you'll have records."

He sighs disappointedly as he looks at all of us.

Wicked steps up to the dining table, "No apology needed, boss. We knew the repercussions, and you saved us from doing more than they were going to sentence us to. Being together will help the time go by faster and I think Reap, Demon, and Fiend can agree; having a record only solidifies us more as a badass biker gang!" He laughs and it causes a ripple effect and we're all chuckling.

"To the Merciless Few!"

"Here! Here!"

Avi is not okay with this, but she is holding back her feelings for Raven's sake. I caught her several times wiping away a stray tear from dinner to movie night. I kept whispering affirmations to let her know that we would be alright.

"How do you know, huh?! All I can think is that the most important person and my family are being ripped away from me." She balls her hands up in anger.

"I need you to be strong, Avi, because one of us has to be and I can't guarantee I won't lose it in there. I need you to be my strength and backbone. My vulnerability is hard to admit but the fact is, I need you, Avi."

She seemed surprised at my admission. She forcefully exhales, "Okay. I'll do it for you, for us."

The next day we took the truck to the bookstore to buy Raven a stack of books and the countdown calendar. Avi picked up several books geared toward passing the citizenship test and a few romance novels. She said it'll keep her hopeful that eventually, we'll get our happily ever after.

After dropping them off, the crew heads down to the Sheriff's station to sign the affidavit that this time next week we will turn ourselves in to serve six months at the South Middlesex Correctional Center, which is just over an hour's drive away. We spent the rest of the day in church to wrap up the loose ends. We ended up meeting the Ace of Spades and I was surprised to see Everett but also relieved, they were in good hands.

When we were done night had fallen and Avi was not

happy. She was pissed that we only had so much time left and she planned for us to walk around at sunset. I pulled her outside, the night was quiet and you could hear every bird, cricket, and frog. It was nature's song. You could also see every star in the sky, not one cloud to hide the beauty. She looks at me with the mad look and I stop us. "I'm sorry, I can't control church, but I want you to look up and see that a star walk is as magical as the sunset. And if you feel down, I want you to stand in this very spot," I grab her and she wraps her arms around mine as I kiss her temple, "close your eyes, and hear me when I say that I love you, Avi."

She gasped and spun around to look me in the eyes. She shook her head in disbelief. "I was supposed to say it first." I rock us side to side, "Who cares who says it first as long as you mean it. I don't expect you..."

She jumps up and wraps her legs around me, "I love you. I love you so much!" She's attacking me with kisses all over and I am not going to fight it. It's these memories that'll keep me going.

I realize that the moment is getting intense. She hops off me but pulls me down on top of her in the grassy opening. I can see it in her eyes, lust. I pause and look at her lying in the grass, her hair fanned out and lips begging to be kissed. She slowly pulled her dress up and my eyes followed to reveal she wasn't wearing any underwear. I growled, gripping her hips tight. "What a pleasant surprise. You must want something. Tell me what you want, Avi."

She arched her back and moaned, "I want you to make love to me, right here, right now."

I pull her off-the-shoulder dress down to reveal her breasts, kissing them gently before covering them with my hands while I devour her sensitive nipples so deliciously. I wanted every moment, every movement, and how sweet she tasted on my tongue engrained in my memory. I wanted her moans, her gasps, her cries of my name and I want her to remember these moments. I balance myself on my knees and pull her against me as we connect underneath the stars. It was raw and carnal as she rode me while I tried to balance and simultaneously stimulate her clit. Her dress pooled at her waist, my jeans at my knees to pad them as I stroked her long and deep. Like horny teenagers who couldn't even wait until prom night except this was love. Raw, passionate love.

Four orgasms later she lays against me, "I can't...anymore." I lay her down on her side, facing me, looking her in the eyes as I push her soft body against me, stroking her slowly.

"Yes, you can, darlin'. Just one more, Avi, one more time. Take it for me, I know you can. You're so close." I hold her leg up and lean forward causing me to go deeper than before. "Oh!" She yelped but reassured me, "So close, don't stop."

"You feel so incredible, I can't stop...I can't." She clenches down which sends me overboard. "Fuck, Avi, shit!"

"Cullen." It wasn't a yelp or scream; it wasn't above a whisper as she shook beneath me. Then she broke the silence with a chuckle, "Are you trying to get six months' worth of sex out of me in a week?"

"You make it sound so dirty. I want lasting memories to take with me." I help her dress after she slips on her bra. "I know. I think you were right; the star walk is much better than the sunset but it's cold! Let's get back and snuggle under the covers."

"You think they know?"

"We've been gone over an hour and we're not that far from the house, they could have heard us...so it's pretty safe to say they know. I'm sure they're all going to do the same thing; you know power up their reserve bank."

I gave her ass a smack and it caused a hitch in her step and she looked back with a fire in her eye. I shrugged my shoulders, "What? It's for my reserve." She rolls her eyes, "Oh, brother."

Chapter Forty-Four
Avi

It came too fast and I feel I didn't get enough time to prepare for this moment. It's the most heartbreaking day of my life. I'm standing with him outside the police station where they must turn themselves in.

I guess the good thing is that Frankie has been extradited back to South America to spend his sentence in the Araraquara Prison in São Paulo. I know Frankie would try something if they shared the same space, probably paying someone to do his dirty work like the coward he was, but he was gone and I was free of him.

I hear his watch beep, 4:00 p.m. Then his hand grazes my face, "It's time."

"No."

"The sooner we do this the quicker time will go."

"That's a lie and you know it!" My anger like a heatwave coursing through my body.

"You're my strong girl; both of you are." He looks down at Raven who, surprisingly, isn't crying. He kneels down to her, "You are my big brave girl, right?"

"Right! I'm going to be brave and watch after mama. Don't forget about me..." She hugs him immediately and I feel that lump form again.

"Never, every single day I'll be thinking about my girl... and my daughter." I gasp and he takes my hand, "I promise you after my time is up, I'm going to make all of this right. We're going to have the house and picket fence, maybe even a dog for her to play with. Look to the future, our future Avi. I love you."

I nod knowingly, "I- I love you, too. We love you."

"I love you, *papai*."

He pulls me in by my neck. The kiss is filled with love and hurt, heartache and promise. I squeeze my eyes tight until he breaks the moment and my eyes fill with tears. He steps back slowly, taking one last look at his family. All the women are sniffling as we come together to hug each other for comfort.

"Come on guys, let's get this over with. Sam, my baby girl, I love you." Lucifer winks to lighten this sad occasion.

She only nods, knowing that speaking will cause her to breakdown. I'm the same and I saw tears fall down my little girl's cheeks, it wasn't the last thing I wanted him to see but I hoped it motivated him to get back to us.

Chapter Forty-Five
Reaper

The last thing I saw were the tears of my little girl as the door shut behind me. I was going to make it up to her. I would do my time and create a plan to give her the best life possible.

One month in:

Avi's first visit they kept us separated behind the glass and she seemed to be keeping it together as best she could. She told me how Raven kicked and screamed to come but she didn't want her in a place like this and I agreed. The jail was trauma-tizing enough.

"The girls have been helping me with my studies. We've even turned it into a game night. Why do you have so many Presidents? We've had our same leader for almost my whole life."

"That's not necessarily a good thing, baby. I'm glad you're learning so much, you'll pass that test with flying colors."

"How are you? Are they treating you guys right? Are you in danger?"

"You watch too many movies, darlin'. I'm...adjusting. It's pretty boring and tame, no rival gangs want to jump us or shank us in the showers, okay? I'm really glad to see you." I place my hand against the plexiglass and she does the same and although there was space between us, I could still feel her warmth.

"I love you."

"And I love you. You can do this."

Three months in:

I spend most of my free time in the library learning new skills. Sometimes the guys join me except Demon; he's become a gym rat. Probably to see the twins swoon over his tighter, toned physique. He really is going to lose his balls one day.

We still eat together but we signed up for different jobs around the prison like the laundry room, the print shop, etc. I signed up for a mechanic's course to learn more about troubleshooting bikes and cars. I had mostly fixed Betty girl myself and I enjoyed it. Why not try to make a decent living from it?

I hadn't seen Avi in over a month, stating in a call that she hadn't felt good on visitor's day and the girls were taking care of her. Still, she wanted to keep me encouraged even though she was sick. Hearing her voice over the phone kept me grounded. "You're almost halfway there, baby. It'll be over before you know it. Then it'll be just the three of us."

"You might not recognize me with all this facial hair."

"Ooh, you probably look even sexier. I can't wait to see."

But yet another missed weekend came and went and I was concerned. I called her this time.

"I had to go to the doctor and today was the earliest he was able to see me."

"Are you okay? You've been dealing with this for too long."

"Yes, it's just a stupid bug, I promise. He said it'll take some time to pass."

"As long as you are okay. This might be a sign for you not to come anymore. My time is winding down and honestly, I don't want you in here. This is no place for family."

"What? But I only got to see you a few times..."

"No buts, the next time I see you is when I'm walking out of here, deal?"

She huffs then sighs hard, "If that's what you want then fine."

"Good girl."

Five months and 29 days in:

Tomorrow I taste freedom and I can't sleep. Lucifer called us to a makeshift church.

"I'm proud of my boys for bettering yourselves during your time here. I spoke with Sam and they are overjoyed, and even planned a celebration upon our return. They will meet us outside of the gates at 9 a.m. Knowing them they'll be there at 8:30 a.m. or sleep in the truck." We laugh but we know that it is a real possibility, especially with Sam and Avi coming to claim their men.

I couldn't wait to see Avi! I had prolonged satisfaction by telling her to stay away but now I was bursting at the scams. I would have them run right into my arms and hug them so tightly.

"A lot has been going on, but our brothers have kept them safe. I know you can't wait to get out of here; I'm right there with you. I want you to each write a letter about your time here, you can write it to yourself or someone, but I want you to journal this experience. You made it brothers; as your President, I'm proud of you. Now we have to find a new way to fund the club. Our security services will have to be 100% legit. Nonetheless, here's to my brothers, my family. Here, here."

"Here, here!"

Later, I lay in bed with my hand on my heart, listening to it thump. Every thump closer to when I could lay eyes on my girls. I don't know what time it was, but it was getting lighter outside.

Chief gathered us in holding. "I want to thank you fellas for taking this in stride, I didn't want this, but it was above even my head. Come on, let's get you out of here, gather your things, and sign out. Rocco we'll talk next week about the job."

"Roger that."

I was the last to sign out and grab my belongings before Lucifer walked toward the door to the gates of the prison. Sam, in her shortest shorts, tied-up plaid shirt, and cowboy boots was squealing and jumping up and down until the moment the gate started to open. She sprinted toward him. "Rocco!" He braces for the hit then he picks her up as she pummels him with kisses. She notices his beard is substantially longer as she tugs it. "You like it?"

"I mean it's not bad. I missed you, Bubba!"

We all walk past, allowing them their moment. The twins are here to greet Demon as he lifts them both and their eyes light up at how much stronger he is. I see the bunnies with welcome home signs but I don't see Avi.

Was she still sick? I was starting to worry it was more than she was letting on, then I heard the voice.

"*Papai! Papai!*" There's my little girl hiding behind the sign that Lila was holding. She ran as fast as her little legs could take her right into my arms and I squeezed her so tight. "Ahh, there's my tater tot! I missed you so much. Just as pretty as I remember if not more."

She giggles as she pulls my facial hair, "You look funny! You look like a..umm, a grizzly bear! RAWR!" I brush against her with my beard and she screams for me to stop. I take her hand while walking up to Lil. I hug her while still looking around.

"Where's Avi, is she still sick? Is something wrong? She wouldn't tell me how sick she really was. It's something serious, isn't it?" I sound rattled but it's because I just don't know anything and not knowing makes it worse.

"Cullen," She started and suddenly I felt dread. What had happened? What wasn't she telling me?

Oh God. Avi...

"Ah, hold your horses! Nothing's wrong. It takes me a bit longer to get around with this."

Lo and behold is the love of my life. She slowly came from around the truck when she revealed why she had missed visitation and had to go to the doctor.

She was pregnant...very pregnant.

Everybody went quiet, at least all the guys because of course, the girls knew. All the guys had their mouths wide open much like me.

Raven grabs my hand and tugs, "Mommy's got my baby brother in there!"

I'm stunned and speechless. She was now in front of me, biting her lip because I hadn't reacted. I stared at her bump. I felt like my movements were in slow motion as I raised my hand to touch her and she placed her hand on top of mine.

"A... a baby?"

"A son. Due in several weeks' time, I haven't had the smoothest time, but I didn't want you to worry. They took good care of me while you were here and now..." Her sniffles forced me to look up. She was smiling and bawling, "you're home. I missed you so much, baby!" I fall to my knees, wrapping my arms around her tightly. "I'm sorry, I should have been there. Why didn't you tell me?"

"So, you could worry? It was morning sickness, no worse

than what I had with Raven except for the one week I was bedridden which was before the Dr.'s visit. The girls waited on me hand and foot, especially Lila. Plus, I thought this could be a nice surprise."

"Oh my god! This is the best surprise ever, coming home to my girls and knowing that you and I created...a baby. Wow."

"And you get to name him, so you better start thinking. In the meantime, let's go home. We have a big celebration waiting for you guys."

I rub her stomach and smile. I'm so ready to go home.

Epilogue

Avi

Twelve months later

I know they are safe with their daddy. I love watching them all together in the backyard. Raven rode her purple bike with training wheels around the perimeter, she swears she's ready to take them off but the mommy in me is not ready to see her little girl grow so fast. Cullen is on a blanket playing with his son.

Onyx Harlow Anderson, the minute he told me the name he chose I fell in love with it. It was a kickass biker name if he decided to join his dad's club.

The day after Cullen was released, he handed me a hand-written letter about his time in prison. There were highs and lows, but he always said the thought of us kept him going.

When he returned, he doted on me hand and foot until my water broke at the clubhouse during dinner. If you could see the color drain from his face, from all their faces! Twenty-seven hours later, the moment they saw Onyx they were smitten. He was their first club baby! Sam even made him a tiny biker cut the had the initials RJ, for Reaper, Jr. Being overly emotional I cried because it was so cute! And that's what we put on him for his newborn photos, on a motorcycle, of course.

From time to time, I hear the roar of their engines as they make their way to our house which is only a couple of miles away. Cullen was adamant about making a home for us, especially after the pregnancy was revealed. He got an entry job at the shop that fixed his bike after the crash and now he's one of the shift supervisors. He also still runs security jobs with the rest of the boys. Everything was 100% legit now, Rocco and the Chief managed to talk to some of the suppliers who dock at the port regularly and secure steady security for their shipments.

I used my money to put the down payment up on this place; it was an amazing feeling. He tried to argue but until I could get proper documentation and work, this was my contribution to our life together. He smacked my ass and said, "That's my little spitfire."

I was so lost in my thoughts I didn't even know they came inside until I heard the cutest giggles and felt tiny fingers in my hair. I turn around and snatch him away from his daddy. "There's mama's baby! Did you have fun outside with *sua irmã*? (your sister) Uh oh! Looks like daddy needs to change you first and then it's time to eat. Maybe you'll go down for the night? Hmm? Go to your daddy."

He groaned as I handed him back. "Darlin', come on...he always sprays me!"

"You have the same equipment. You should know how to duck by now. I've never been hit and trust me; the little scoundrel has tried. I'm almost done with dinner and I got to put Raven in the tub, so it's only fair. Besides, I thought I would treat my dearest fiancé to a deep tissue massage since he's been working hard, doing double shifts, and working with his brothers to make a comfortable life for us."

He growls with Onyx in his arms, leaning in for a quick kiss, "Keep talking. You might get knocked up again." With that, he walks away. I look down to see Raven on her kitchen stand where she helps me cook.

"What can I do, mama?" Her English has improved so much and this year she started first grade. During our first parent-teacher conference the teacher told me if she continued excelling, she would recommend Raven for the accelerated program. It was exciting to hear that after all she had been through, nothing would stop her from being someone great!

"You peel the eggs for the salad and then get the wooden bowl and dressing out of the fridge. All while you tell me the planets of the solar system."

"Yes, mama. There's Mars, the red planet and then Jupiter, which has rings around it! Earth, where we live, Venus..." Her voice fades as I think about the freedom she has now that she never had before. She can go to school and learn. I made sure I got her papers in so she could get a school ID and benefit from the lunch program. She can enjoy her school's library, she spends so much time in there I was worried she was isolating herself, but she tells me she knows plenty of kids and she has best friends, Rosa and Kimberly. She even asked if she could invite them over for a sleepover. It was an experience I never had but I will live through her when she does. She wants a dinosaur-themed sleepover, her newest obsession. And most importantly, we don't have to look over our shoulders anymore for fear the boogeyman will come back and kill us.

Word got back to the son, who lived in Armenia, that his father was viciously killed by Frankie and the son had enough power to have him murdered in prison. Rumors are that he actually paid the security guards to slit his throat but knowing how corrupt the system is there, I wouldn't be surprised. They wrote it off as an unfortunate incident and no one was charged.

The details were gruesome and I didn't relay it to Raven, I only told her that Uncle Frankie had an accident and he was now in Heaven. She didn't even react but later she told me she said a prayer for her uncle so he could be at peace. That was very mature of her. Honestly, he was probably burning in Hell but she didn't need any more bad memories. It's bittersweet. I never wanted Frankie to die. I wanted my brother not the monster of greed that took over.

I told Cullen when we were able, I would take him down to Maua; he said he wanted to know all of me, the good and the bad, and that includes returning home. Maybe I can visit Frankie's grave. I made sure to have him buried next to our parents. I wanted to finally forgive him and not have the burden of anger at someone who is no longer alive; I won't give him the power.

Epilogue
Reaper

Onyx, once again, tries to mark me but I shift to the right in time and now he's laughing innocently. "Nice try, buddy. Your old man is quick! Can you say Da Da? Da Da!"

He squeals as I tickle him, trying to escape the changing station but I put his clothes back on and we go sit at the island. My tater tot loves helping her mom with cooking. Maybe she'll grow up to be a world-star chef or perhaps a librarian since she loves bookstores and the library. There isn't a weekend she doesn't ask to go. She's going to have her own library soon. Whatever it is, I love the fact that I can be there to watch her grow.

It's been a long, hard road. I didn't think I'd ever love anyone after Daisy, who's currently serving time for Avi's drugging. She only got eight years, but she'll be irrelevant by the time she's released. And if she knew what's good for her, she'd skipped town after. Avi's still looking to rearrange her face in the most painful way possible.

Anyway, my life turned on its side, literally when I slid across that asphalt. Scarred for life and scared to ride again but when push came to shove, I hopped on, put my boots in the wind, and rode in to save the day. I'm not on my Betty girl as much as I used to be, but I think she understands that I'm a family man now and that the SUV is more practical.

But some days Avi nudges me outside, "Why don't you take Betty girl out and link up with the guys? It's been a while, who knows maybe one day I'll get a bike for myself."

I pull her toward me and smile, "That would be amazing."

I start her up as I look at my family who saved me from my wreck of a life. I rev her three times for the heartbeats of my life. I have my brothers to thank for this.

The Merciless Few forever.

The End

A million thanks to my fellow Merciless Few authors for allowing me to accompany you on this journey and this 'brotherhood'. I am forever thankful for you, our MF members, and readers.

Look out for other releases from the rest of the Merciless Few authors!

Where to find me:
Linktr.ee: https://linktr.ee/mskeiya
Website: https://www.scourtneybooks.com/
FB: https://facebook.com/shakkia.courtney
IG: https://www.instagram.com/author_mskeiya
Twitter: https://www.twitter.com/author_mskeiya

From S. Courtney

Thank you for taking the time to read Sandman. I hope you enjoyed the book and would love if you could leave a review on any retailer or Goodreads.

If you would like to hear more from me about new releases and sales, you can visit my website.

Website: https://www.scourtneybooks.com/